Hunter's Moon

Hunter Lane Chandler returns to Rattlesnake Valley with fresh game to sell to the townsfolk only to discover the town is seemingly empty. In the sheriff's office, he finds the veteran lawman has been killed. Then in the livery stable he finds the slaughtered body of the blacksmith.

Soon he finds out that a deadly bunch of outlaws known as Corbin's Raiders have not only killed several of the townsfolk, but have also taken schoolteacher Molly Drew with them.

Chandler sets out to rescue Molly. But he soon finds out that hunting men is a far more dangerous than hunting animals.

Please return / renew this item HW
by the last date shown.
Books may also be renewed by
phone or the Internet.

Tel: 01204 332384

www.bolton.gov.uk/libraries

Hunter's Moon

Ty Walker

A Black Horse Western

ROBERT HALE

© Ty Walker 2017
First published in Great Britain 2017

ISBN 978-0-7198-2499-9

The Crowood Press
The Stable Block
Crowood Lane
Ramsbury
Marlborough
Wiltshire SN8 2HR

www.bhwesterns.com

Robert Hale is an imprint
of The Crowood Press

The right of Ty Walker to be identified as
author of this work has been asserted by him
in accordance with the Copyright, Designs and
Patents Act 1988

Typeset by
Derek Doyle & Associates, Shaw Heath
Printed and bound in Great Britain by
CPI Group (UK) Ltd, Croydon, CR0 4YY

Dedicated to my friend Stuart Wall

PROLOGUE

It was as though every animal within the forested terrain knew what was moving slowly toward them through its confines. Death has an acrid aroma that always travels with those who unleash its execution. It is a stench that all the forest creatures, even the boldest, recognize and try to avoid. The wildlife had fled to safer ground long before the horsemen reached them.

The eight riders emerged from the morning mist like phantoms and cut down through the rocky confines on their way to the remote settlement of Rattlesnake Valley. The town lay in the centre of a flat dusty gorge and had been named by the first mountain men who used it as a meeting area. At one time a French company had a string of trading outposts and bought the furs and pelts which the burly mountain men brought to them. It had been a lucrative trade for many decades but when the vast tracts of land were eventually sold to the ever-expanding American government, the outposts disappeared and so did the sturdy men who had tamed the wilderness. Hunters and trappers were a dying breed of men and for the most part had vanished without trace. Apart from the odd resilient soul, they were gone.

Rattlesnake Valley had survived because it was on the stagecoach route. A vital link between more civilized towns that lay beyond the still-hostile terrain that flanked the scattering of wooden structures.

The eight horsemen neither knew nor cared anything about the history of the town they were approaching. They had another motive for being in this area. A reason which had brought them over three hundred miles across a parched prairie and into the forested hills that led down toward the place known simply as Rattlesnake.

The riders moved in single file like the cavalry they had once been. They did not utter a word as they guided their horses between the rugged rocks on their way to their destination.

This was like a military operation. The lead rider had planned its every detail with the same precision that he had used during the brutal war and the years that had followed.

Colt Corbin had never surrendered. His troop of

equally vicious followers had refused to yield to the men in Union uniforms. That was not their way.

Since the war had ended, there were many men like themselves who refused to become subservient to their northern enemies. Slowly their numbers had diminished, but their hatred was no less fiery.

They would continue fighting their enemies until their own lives were snuffed out. They all had lost everything during the war and knew that it was pointless to return to their homes because they no longer existed.

Corbin's Raiders, as they had been tagged, would continue to bring their own brand of vengeance to anyone who got in their way. They would rob and kill with the same mindless skill that had been drilled into them before being sent into the jaws of war.

The war had taught them to become expert and emotionless killers. It had taught them to feel nothing but contempt for their enemies; and as far as Corbin and his men were concerned, that meant every man, woman and child they encountered. Mercy was something that none of them recognized any longer. Hate had devoured every other emotion until it was the only thing that remained in their putrid souls.

Water lapped over the hoofs of their mounts as they reached the fast-flowing river. Corbin dragged on his long leathers, turned his mount, jabbed his spurs and continued along the bank of the river.

If pure evil could be envisaged, it was the sight of the heavily armed horsemen as they trailed trustingly behind Colt Corbin.

Although Corbin had never been to this land before, he led his men toward the remote town with dogged expertise. Although none of the eight men could see beyond the trees that loomed over their caravan, they trusted that Corbin knew where it was and where they were headed.

There were no doubts in Corbin's mind as to where Rattlesnake was. He had studied many maps before setting out on this quest and it was branded into his cold and calculating mind. It was like a magnet dragging him on to Rattlesnake. His dishevelled followers trailed the tail of his high-shouldered mount as they had always done. Corbin was that rarity among military leaders and always led from the front.

Like so many other highly-decorated soldiers, Corbin was unafraid of death. He would lead his men with no thought for his own mortality and this had made him far more trusted than his contemporaries. Corbin was said to never send any of his loyal followers into the jaws of death without riding at their head. Even though, unlike normal men, his twisted mind had no sense of morality, he had never once forsaken his now sparse army.

As his mount continued along the riverbank, the morning light began to filter through the tree canopies. Corbin sniffed the air like a bloodhound. He looked over his shoulder at the men as he pushed a cigar into the corner of his mouth.

'We're getting close, men,' he growled as his thumbnail scratched a match into flame. 'My nose tells me we should get there in the next hour.'

The riders behind his broad back nodded and casually saluted Corbin. He inhaled the strong smoke and then allowed it to filter between his gritted teeth. He raised an arm and signalled to the deadly horsemen to follow.

The eight horsemen continued on toward their goal.

ONE

The mist hung a foot above the ground as the morning sun crept between the buildings of the small settlement. Few of the townsfolk were awake this close to sun-up, but those that were moved along the sidewalks in readiness of the new day. Long shadows began to slowly shrink as the blazing sun chased them away. None of those who had rubbed the sleep from their eyes noticed the line of horse-men who snaked out of the trees above the large livery stable at the end of the remote town and moved steadily toward it.

The mist, which shimmered like a plague of phan-toms, concealed the deadly eight horsemen as they rode slowly through the frosty air.

Corbin led his band of vicious raiders as he always did in the chilling silence, which was his custom. His eyes darted along the main street and then returned to the tall livery stable, which he had decided was their starting point.

Had anybody cast their attention upon the trailing riders, they would have instantly realized that they were no ordinary bunch of outlaws. Each of them still sported the physical memories of the war. Parts of their once pristine grey uniforms still remained, but time had ravaged them. Only the arsenal of weaponry they all carried showed no signs of wear and tear. The dishevelled riders had continued their own personal war even though the hostilities had long since ceased. Where once they had only attacked and killed those they regarded as Union soldiers or sympathizers, now they waged their brutality against everyone they encountered.

They had learned their lethal trade well.

Probably too well.

What had once been an honourable troop of well-trained soldiers fighting for a just cause had become nothing more than a ravaged bunch of men killing for the sheer lust of it. Revenge is a sinister companion. It is like a drug. It overwhelms and devours those who use it as an excuse.

Corbin raised his right hand and then slowly stopped his mount outside the closed barn doors of the livery. His seven followers pulled back on their long leathers beside the brooding Corbin.

'Open them doors and we'll take these nags inside

the stable, boys,' Corbin muttered as he dismounted and looked along the street. The rising mist was still shielding them from curious eyes. 'I don't want any of the town's nosy-parkers seeing us until I'm ready.'

Like a well-oiled machine, the outlaws followed his orders to the letter. Within seconds they had opened the tall stable doors and led all eight of their horses into the dark interior of the lofty structure.

Corbin swung on his boots and marched in after them.

He paused, rested his knuckles on his gun belt and stared into the depths of the large building.

The burly blacksmith Mort Riley did not usually rise before nine, but the sound of his unexpected visitors suddenly woke him. He rolled off the pile of hay in an empty stall and yawned as he slowly pulled on his boots.

'How'd you get in here?' Riley asked as he stood up and looked at the eight men in the middle of the livery. 'I could have sworn I locked them doors.'

'You did,' Corbin said bluntly as he slowly walked toward the muscular blacksmith. 'But there ain't a lock that can stop my boys.'

Riley tilted his head back and squinted at Corbin. He was confused by the statement. 'What do you fellas want?'

Corbin sighed and pushed his hat off his temple.

'We just wanted to get our nags off the street,' he

replied as he pulled a cigar from his coat pocket and bit off its tip. 'They need grain and water. I figured that this was the best place to find it.'

Riley grinned, 'Damn right, stranger. I got more grain in here than anywhere in the whole territory.'

'That's fine,' Corbin smiled. It was not a smile like most folks display when happy or amused. It was a dark, dangerous smile, created in the bowels of his heartless innards. 'Feed our nags.'

The face of Mort Riley suddenly went ashen. He nodded and moved the horses as every one of the outlaws' eyes burned into him. He suddenly became aware that the men who had invaded his livery were not the usual type he was used to. They were dressed in clothing that harked back to the Confederacy and had more weapons than he had ever seen any men carrying.

He hung a feed bag over Corbin's mount's head and then started to gather more bags together. 'I ain't seen you in these parts before, have I?'

Corbin struck a match and inhaled. 'I surely doubt it.'

Riley began scooping grain from a sack into one of the canvas bags as he noticed the strangers gathering around him like a pack of timber wolves.

'I reckon you boys must be passing through Rattlesnake,' the large figure joked. 'Nobody ever comes here on purpose. They're usually heading somewhere interesting.'

Corbin blew out the flame and dropped the match onto on to the sod floor. He then moved to the glowing forge and allowed its warmth to take the ache out of his bones.

'This is where we were heading,' he said through a cloud of smoke. 'Rattlesnake Valley.'

Riley stopped filling the bags and stared at Corbin.

'You come here on purpose?' he gasped.

'We sure did,' Corbin turned to face the blacksmith, with the cigar gritted in his teeth. Again he smiled the same sickly smile.

Riley straightened up and hauled the heavy bags to the rest of the horses. He began hanging the bags over each of the horse's heads in turn as he pondered the statement. Finally curiosity outweighed caution. He looked at Corbin.

'Why in hell would anybody come to this town?' he asked the outlaw leader. 'Are you serious? You come here on purpose?'

Corbin moved away from the forge. A trail of cigar smoke hung over his shoulder as he closed the distance on the bewildered blacksmith. 'Tell me,' he drawled. 'Is there a young gal in Rattlesnake named Molly Drew?'

Riley raised his eyebrows. 'Did you come visiting her?'

Corbin looked to two of his men and nodded.

16

They swiftly moved in behind the burly man and grabbed his arms. Riley struggled for a few moments until his eyes saw the look which was carved across Corbin's face.

'Answer my damn question,' Corbin growled as his teeth chewed on the cigar angrily. 'Is there a gal in this town called Molly Drew?'

Riley nodded fearfully, 'Yep. She runs the school.'

Corbin snapped his fingers. His men released their grip on the blacksmith and backed away. Riley pushed his thick fingers through the loose strands of his hair. He was angry, but knew only too well that these men meant business.

'How many guns are there in this town?' Corbin asked as he pulled the cigar from his lips and tapped the ash on to the floor.

'Not many,' Riley answered without thinking.

Corbin nodded as he blew a line of smoke at the floor. 'Do you have one?'

The large blacksmith straightened up. For the first time since he had been suddenly awoken, Riley sensed the danger he was in. His eyes moved between the outlaws and then returned to Corbin. He swallowed hard and felt his heart pounding inside his chest like an Apache war drum. He continued to feed the horses as his mind raced.

'All I got is an old scattergun,' Riley replied.

'Who else has a gun?' Corbin pressed.

17

Riley knew that he had to escape before they turned their wrath on him. But the harder he racked his brain, the more confused he became.

'The sheriff has one,' Riley gulped. 'A few other folks got guns, but nobody ever uses them. The sheriff is the only critter to actually wear one.'

Corbin turned and looked at his men.

'This is gonna be easier than I figured, boys,' he stated.

Riley stopped in his tracks. He bit his lower lip nervously and edged toward the leader of the outlaws. He could feel his expectation of life disappearing with every breath he took.

'Why'd you ask about Molly?' he wondered.

Corbin pulled his heavy jacket back until it revealed his holster and sabre scabbard. He looked at the large inquisitive blacksmith through a veil of cigar smoke.

'Where would she be at this time of day?' Corbin growled and rested his hand on the hilt of his scabbard. His eyes were like fiery orbs as they glared at Riley. 'Tell me.'

Riley glanced at the outlaws and then raised a shaking hand and pointed far beyond the scattering of wooden structures that made up the remote township. All eight outlaws stared long and hard at the single-storey building set on the other side of Rattlesnake.

'There,' the big man stammered. 'That's the school house.'

Corbin pulled the cigar from his lips and glared at the blacksmith. A cruel grin emerged from behind the week-old stubble as he flicked the ash on to the straw-covered ground.

'Cut out and saddle a horse, big fella,' he growled. 'One suited to Molly's little frame.'

Riley frowned. 'Are you taking her with you?'

'That's right,' Corbin replied before inhaling hard on his cigar and then blowing the smoke into the face of the blacksmith. 'Any objections?'

All Riley could do was twitch as he shrugged and moved to the stalls and led out a handsome horse. He patted the shoulder of the animal and then tossed a blanket on to its shoulders. As his large hands dragged a saddle off the stall poles, he felt his heart pounding even harder inside his massive chest. Riley wanted to snap each and every one of their necks before they unleashed their venomous fury on the unsuspecting souls in Rattlesnake, but he knew that men who were as well armed as this bunch knew exactly how to use their weaponry.

A bead of sweat trailed down his face as he heaved the saddle on to the horse's back. As he reached under the horses belly and retrieved the cinch strap, he wondered how he was going to warn the town.

He tightened the strap and tucked its slack under

the blanket before lowering the fender down. Riley had no sooner finished saddling the horse when Corbin moved toward him.

Riley stared into the expressionless face as it approached. He tried to swallow but there was no spittle to lubricate his throat.

'What now?' he asked in a shaking tone.

The question had only just left his lips when he saw the outlaw leader pull the sabre from its scabbard. The blacksmith ran to the far end of the livery stable but Corbin followed with the gleaming blade at his side.

Riley shook his hands as his back pressed up against the far wall.

'What you doing?'

The question was answered without words.

A simple thrust of the deadly sword caught the larger man dead centre. A choking whimper rattled from the blacksmith as the long blade went straight through him.

Corbin stared at the startled and terrified face of the big man as he slumped to the ground. Blood squirted from the hideous wound as Corbin pulled his sabre free of the stricken blacksmith and then casually wiped the crimson evidence on a horse blanket.

It was as though he had swatted a fly and not destroyed the life of an innocent man. A smirk traced his face as he satisfied himself that the blade was back to its pristine best.

Corbin slid the gleaming blade back into its scabbard and turned to look at his chuckling men. He paced back toward their grinning faces and then threw his cigar on to the forge.

He stopped and glanced out at the long street. None of the locals realized the outrage that just occurred at the very edge of Rattlesnake. That suited the outlaws.

Corbin raised his hand to shield his eyes from the sun and studied the unsuspecting townsfolk. The seven men behind him were eager to continue the mayhem. They could smell the blood their leader had just spilled. Corbin was here for a purpose, but if it meant killing the entire population of the remote town to achieve that goal, then so be it.

Corbin looked at the street as though he were facing a potential battlefield. He rested his knuckles on his hips and lowered his head until his chin touched his tunic collar.

'Now we can begin,' he muttered.

TWO

Sheriff Seth Brown would have been regarded as far too old to wear a tin star in most other towns or cities in the West, but not Rattlesnake. The peaceful settlement had never had any real trouble in all its history so none of the residents worried that Brown was getting a tad long in the tooth. His mettle had never been tested. Brown had spent the previous eleven years going about his daily business and giving every living soul within the confines of the remote town a sense of safety.

He had awoken as usual at dawn and moved from the vacant jail cell into the body of his office. This small place had become his home since he had first pinned on the tin star and vowed to protect Rattlesnake Valley from any potential danger that might arise.

Seth Brown had no way of knowing it, but this was

the day when that danger would raise its head. The veteran lawman dried his face and then shuffled across the office to the door and opened it. He tossed the bowl of water into the sand as was his habit and inhaled the fresh morning air. His eyes darted around the street and, when content that everything was as it should be, he ambled back to his stove and set the coffee pot on his stove.

He sat down at his desk and dragged his boots on.

As the seasons had passed over the years and he had grown increasingly older, Brown had become more and more complacent. Before his hair had turned to the colour of snow, he would never have allowed anyone to see him without his six-gun strapped around his ample girth. Now he often forgot to wear his holstered .45 at all.

The elderly lawman yawned and rubbed his eyes. He then moved to the wall clock and pushed the small black key into the clock face and wound it up. He pushed the small key into his pants pocket and then closed the glass cover on the clock.

Brown rubbed his belly and bit his whiskered lip.

'The café ain't gonna open up for another hour yet,' he grumbled as his weathered hands lifted his black vest off the back of his chair and slid it on. He breathed on the tin star and polished it with his sleeve.

As he caught his reflection in the glass front of the

23

clock, a smile filled his face. The star still filled him with pride, even though the sight of what he had become was less pleasing.

'I'll take me a walk around town to keep the folks happy and with any luck they'll open the café,' he grinned and nodded to himself. 'That's what I'll do. Make old Hyram in the café think it's later than it really is.'

Brown plucked his hat off a stack of wanted circulars and placed it over his mane of silver locks. His hands smoothed the sides of his Stetson and then he turned toward the door.

Before the veteran lawman had taken a step toward the open doorway the sound of spurs rang out along the boardwalk. Brown stopped and straightened up as a shadowy figure passed the solitary window of the sheriff's office.

Brown watched as the daunting figure of Colt Corbin swung on his boot leather and stared into the confines of the office. The far older man squinted as his eyes vainly tried to work out who he was staring at.

Corbin entered without invitation and touched the brim of his hat as he closed the door behind him. The outlaw leader glanced at the sheriff and then moved to the desk and studied the posters littering its surface. He looked up at Brown.

'Have you read any of these, Sheriff?' he asked.

Brown turned toward the stranger, 'Who are you, stranger?'

Corbin smiled.

'So you ain't read any of these Wanted posters.'

Seth Brown licked his lips thoughtfully and edged slowly toward the large man in the hefty top coat. The closer he got, the more he recognized the once familiar uniform. Brown halted his progress and rubbed his chin and neck.

'How come you're wearing a rebel tunic, friend?' he asked the outlaw leader. 'It's kinda faded, but I can still make out the detailing.'

Corbin inhaled and appeared to grow taller as he stood beside the desk. His glare focused on the man wearing the shiny tin star.

'Are you all the law this town's got, old man?' he growled as his hands fanned the posters apart as he studied them. 'Maybe you've a deputy hidden around here someplace. Have you?'

Seth Brown smiled, 'Hell, I'm the only lawman for a hundred miles. Least ways, that's what folks tell me.'

'The only lawman in a hundred miles, huh?' Corbin started to nod as though he had learned enough from the aged lawman. He stepped back from behind the desk and looked at Brown in the same way that a mountain lion eyes its prey.

A sudden dread overwhelmed Brown as the realization of potential danger swept over him like a tidal wave crashing on to a shoreline. His hands patted his hips and then he realized that he had forgotten to lift his holster and gun off the hat rack. His eyes darted to the weathered leather gun belt hanging with its heavy six-shooter cradled in its holster.

Corbin noticed the lawman's eyes staring at the hat rack behind him in the corner. He looked over his shoulder at the gun in its holster hanging on its belt. Corbin then returned his attention to Brown. The veteran star-packer was visibly shaken by his potentially deadly oversight. He wiped his sweating palms against his pants.

The outlaw leader pointed at the holstered gun suspended in its leather cradle and raised a bushy eyebrow.

'Reckon you forgot to strap your gun on, old timer,' he drawled and then pushed the gun. It rocked back and forth like a deadly pendulum. 'You must be even older than you look to be that forgetful.'

Brown gritted his teeth. He considered running, but knew that had ceased to be an option long before he had originally pinned the tin star on. His legs had just about the strength to support his weight nowadays. He licked his dry lips and eyed the merciless rebel raider.

'Who are you?' he repeated.

Corbin picked up one of the posters and turned it

so that his picture faced the lawman. He then pointed at his name and then his image on the thick card.

'This is who I am, Sheriff,' he taunted. 'I'm wanted dead or alive and worth five thousand greenbacks. I'm probably the most valuable critter you've ever met.'

Seth Brown leaned forward and squinted. He did not straighten back up until he had read every single word on the circular. His watery eyes looked into the cruel features of the infamous rebel.

'You're Colt Corbin?' he stammered as he recalled the many torrid tales he had read and heard about concerning the brutal figure before him. Tales that did not seem so far-fetched any longer.

The outlaw nodded and tossed the poster at the wall and advanced toward the sheriff. He stopped a mere six inches away from the shaking lawman and stared at Brown long and hard. He was like a cat tormenting a cornered mouse.

'How come you seem so fearful, Sheriff?' he asked the frightened and confused Brown. 'Have you heard about me?'

Fear rippled through Brown as his terrified mind tried to think of an answer that might not get him killed. He cleared his throat and looked sheepishly at the floorboards.

'Everybody knows about Colt Corbin,' he

somehow managed to croak as his eyes noticed the weapon-laden gun belt and the hilt of the sabre hidden under the grey top coat. 'I've read about you and your raiders.'

'You've heard how we slaughter everything that gets in our way, old timer?' Corbin snarled and started to chuckle. 'All them stories are true. We do what we want and nobody has ever managed to stop us.'

Brown felt his heart quicken. 'I ain't no hero. I'll not try and stop you or your boys from doing whatever you want in Rattlesnake. Just do what you gotta do and ride out of here.'

Corbin shook his head and paced around the sheriff.

'Hell, I'd do that anyway. The thing is I'm here for a special reason, old timer.' The outlaw snarled. The heat of his breath traced over Brown's freshly-scrubbed neck. 'I got me a notion that you know why I'm in this godforsaken town.'

Seth Brown cleared his throat again. He knew all about the infamous Confederate rebel and his band of cutthroats. It had been him that the secret service had confided in when they had brought Corbin's daughter into Rattlesnake Valley. Brown had been sworn to secrecy and vowed that he would never reveal her true identity to anyone. No one was meant to know that Molly Drew was really Molly Corbin.

Yet somehow Colt Corbin knew.

How?

The question burned like a branding iron into the sheriff's fevered mind as he vainly tried to summon the courage he once had in abundance.

'I'm just scared, Corbin,' Brown stammered. 'You are kinda famous and I'm just an old lawman. You got me, soldier. I'm plumb scared and I admit it.'

Corbin grabbed the sheriff's shirt front and dragged it close. So close that the law officer could feel every word that spluttered from the outlaw's mouth.

'Where's my Molly?' he rasped in a torrent of spittle.

Brown swallowed hard, 'I don't know any Molly.'

The expression on Corbin's twisted face went even more threatening as he hauled the older man closer. The veins pulsated on the outlaw's temple as his eyes burned into the old lawman.

'You'd best tell me the truth or I'll gut you like a goddam fish, Sheriff,' the deranged rebel snarled before shaking Brown violently. 'Spill the beans or I'll retire you permanently. Savvy?'

Sweat rolled down Brown's wrinkled face, 'Look, I don't know anything about your daughter. I don't know anything.'

Corbin released his grip, took a step backward and stared straight into the eyes of the veteran lawman.

The maniacal smile erupted over his face. He raised a hand and jabbed his fingers into Brown's chest.

'Now who said anything about Molly being my daughter, Sheriff?' he hissed like a sidewinder warning that he was about to strike. 'I sure didn't say she was my daughter, old timer. How'd you know that if you've no idea who my Molly is?'

Seth Brown backed away from the lethal outlaw nervously. A million thoughts raced through his ancient brain as the dark-souled figure edged toward him. He waved his hands in an attempt to keep Corbin at bay but it was impossible. The old lawman kept staggering backwards until his back touched the wall. He stopped and watched as the rebel leader closed in on him like a raging buffalo.

'Didn't you say she was your daughter?' Brown bluffed.

'Nope,' Corbin shook his head at the trapped lawman. 'I never said she was my daughter so you must know about her, Sheriff. Is my information right about her being the school teacher in this damn town?'

The expression on Brown's face answered the question long before his mouth was able to open. Corbin raised his left hand and smothered the whiskered features as he shook his head.

'You'd best quit while you're ahead, old timer.' He snarled and looked out of the window as his hand smothered the lawman's mouth. 'Them wrinkled old eyes of yours just told me the truth. She is here teaching school just like I was told.'

Brown mustered every scrap of his dwindling strength and freed his mouth.

'She ain't here in Rattlesnake,' he gasped.

Suddenly without warning, Corbin's shoulder dropped and he threw the entire right side of his bulk at the sheriff. Brown felt the powerful blow. It buckled him. He was winded. Then a dull pain in his guts rippled through his aged body as the outlaw stepped back from him.

As Corbin halted three feet away from him, Brown's watery eyes could see his right fist clearly. Yet it was not a clenched fist at all. It was a hand holding something bathed in crimson gore.

Seth Brown suddenly realized that he had not been punched at all, he had been stabbed. Corbin had thrust a long-bladed Bowie knife into him. The sheriff stared in disbelief at the knife as lumps of his innards dripped from its blade and collected in a puddle at his feet. Reluctantly the sheriff slowly looked down at the blood that poured from the hideous wound in his gut.

'Oh my God,' Brown gasped. He tried to continue but the only thing that came from his mouth was blood. It gushed from between his store-bought teeth and flowed down his blood-splattered shirt.

The aged sheriff staggered forward but his executioner placed his free hand on Brown's shoulder to steady him. The grinning outlaw wiped the scarlet gore off his knife blade and then stepped aside and allowed Brown to fall on to the floor.

Corbin looked down at the pathetic sight and then spat at the sheriff. He opened the office door and stepped out into the street as his men rode from the livery stable with his horse and a spare mount.

'We slit the throats of the nags in the stable, Colt,' a grim-featured Fred Katt told his boss. 'A couple of the boys are circling this town making sure that there ain't a living horse or mule left.'

'Good,' Corbin grunted. 'We don't want any of these varmints getting brave and trailing us when we've left.'

Another of the raiders levelled his mount and looked at his emotionless leader as Corbin pulled a cigar from his deep pocket and placed it between his teeth. 'Have we got time to have us some fun, Colt?'

Corbin scratched a match down the wooden upright next to him and cupped its erupting flame as he sucked smoke into his lungs. 'Rustle up as much grub and liquor as you can carry in your saddlebags and follow me.'

'Where you going?' Katt asked Corbin as the outlaw leader grabbed his reins and stepped into his stirrup. Every one of his men watched as Corbin slowly mounted and gathered in his loose leathers.

'I'm headed to the school,' Corbin replied drily as he exhaled a cloud of smoke into the morning air. 'I got me a daughter to round up.'

'You gonna learn her that it don't pay ruffling Colt Corbin's feathers?' Katt grinned through his busted teeth.

'I sure am, Fred,' Corbin replied through even more cigar smoke. 'I'm gonna make sure she learns that nobody runs out on me without paying a darn heavy price.'

Jango Bodine, another of Corbin's followers, stared around the street at the curious townsfolk who were eyeing them from every vantage point around the main street. The heavily armed rebel glanced at them all with a cruel smile carved into his embattled face.

'Can we have us some fun while you round up that filly, Colt?' he repeated his fellow outlaw's question. 'I'm just hankering to kill me a few folks.'

'Some of these womenfolk sure look ripe for the taking,' a heavily-scarred outlaw known only as Trooper Bo added. 'It'd sure be a shame to kill any of them before we has a wrestle.'

Corbin gave a belly laugh, 'I don't give a damn what you do with them, boys. You can kill and bed all of them as far as I'm concerned. Just make sure we've got grub and whiskey for the trail.'

The riders gave out a unified howl of expectant glee and spread out on their mounts. It did not take too long before there was the sound of females screaming and male protests being silenced by gunshots. Gunshots that echoed around the weathered wooden structures in sickening repetition.

Corbin did not appear to notice the females who vainly raced across the street around him as his men chased them atop their lathered-up mounts like wranglers chasing stray steers. The heartless Confederate leader held his reins in his hands and held on to the long leathers of the horse that had been readied for his daughter. He was about to spur when an outraged man ran out before his high-shouldered horse shaking his fists and cursing. Corbin drew one of his six-shooters and squeezed its trigger.

As the bullet hit him in the neck, the man span on his heels and fell in a crumpled heap a few yards ahead of his horse. Corbin pulled back on the hammer of his smoking .45 again and fired another shot into the stricken body.

The body shook and then sank heavily into the sand as a pool of blood spread out around it. Corbin smiled and holstered his smoking gun.

'That'll teach him,' he growled, with the cigar gripped between his teeth, and slapped the tails of his reins against the shoulders of his tall horse. The powerful animal reared up and then started to canter along the main street as its master balanced in his stirrups.

A trail of cigar smoke hung in the air and trailed over his shoulder as Corbin slowly headed to the far end of Rattlesnake Valley. The place where he knew his unsuspecting daughter was working. A rage simmered in his guts as he pulled the brim of his grey hat down to shield his eyes against the rising sun. Corbin felt betrayed by Molly. How could his own flesh and blood turn to the authorities and flee?

The thought grew no calmer.

With each stride of his mount, the sound of mayhem grew louder behind his wide shoulders. A satisfied smirk traced his hardened features as he heard his men starting to paint the town red.

Red with the blood of innocents.

Corbin straightened the army top coat and line of ribbons stitched to its breast pocket as though they belonged to him and he had been decorated during the war. Yet none of it belonged to him. He had stolen it all from a true hero just before he and his troop of raiders were due to submit to the indignity of defeat.

The war had created many monsters, yet Colt Corbin was already a twisted soul long before the conflict. Fighting and killing without fear of punishment had become like a drug to the depraved souls who refused to stop. For years they had ridden and raided with impunity.

His depravity had grown like a cancer.

It was all he and his band of raiders knew. They had turned their individual skills to profitable use since the war officially ceased and would continue doing so until the last of them encountered the Grim Reaper.

As his men continued to cause havoc, Corbin rode on toward the small school situated at the outskirts of Rattlesnake Valley. The louder the screams became, the wider his sickly grin stretched across his unshaven face.

Rattlesnake Valley was a long way from where the war had raged, yet now its townsfolk were being treated to a taste of the horrors they had been fortunate enough to have been spared.

For the first time in its existence the remote settlement was sampling its own war. Suddenly without warning the innocent inhabitants of Rattlesnake were being treated to the bitter bloodshed and brutality for which Corbin's Raiders were infamous.

With the cigar still gripped in his teeth, the horseman caught a glimpse of his goal. The small single-storey structure surrounded by a white picket fence.

'The school,' Corbin drooled.

THREE

The beautiful female, who everyone within the confines of Rattlesnake Valley knew as Molly Drew, sprang to her feet from behind her desk inside the small school building. The sound of horrific gunshots and pitiful screams rang out in the morning air and wafted into the small school building. She alone recognized the sound of death as it resonated around the interior of the tiny structure. Molly glanced at her pupils and could see the confused bewilderment in the children's innocent faces.

The eleven children aged between seven and thirteen looked at the handsome woman as she moved swiftly between their desks to the solitary door in the single roomed school.

After taking a deep breath, Molly released its catch and pulled it toward her so that there was a three-inch gap that she could peer out through.

The glaring sun dazzled her eyes for a few

moments as she stood beside the door and gazed out into the normally quiet street. She recognized the sickening sound that she had heard many times before. The haunting screams of terrified females and the sound of six-guns being blasted at anything that stood in the way of their barrels chilled her to the bone. Deep in her soul Molly knew exactly who was creating so much mayhem in the normally peaceful settlement.

She had thought that her new name and new life in the remote town of Rattlesnake would put an end to the fear and heartbreak that she had suffered all her life. That had been before the shooting had started.

As one of her pale hands tightly gripped the door, the other rose up and shielded her eyes against the brilliant sunshine. Dust mixed with the morning dew as the rays of the merciless sun beat down on the school building, making it nearly impossible to see anything beyond the picket fence that separated the school from the rest of Rattlesnake. Yet Molly kept staring to where she could hear the screams and gunshots in a vain hope that she might get a glimpse of those who were responsible.

There was a slim part of her that prayed it was some other gang of misfits that had descended on Rattlesnake, yet in her heart she knew the truth.

It had to be the evil Corbin and his equally brutal

raiders who were torturing the mostly unarmed residents, she thought. No other creature this side of Hell itself would have shown up in this remote settlement and started to unleash his own brand of insane violence.

Only Corbin.

Only her father.

A cold shiver went through her as she listened to the pathetic cries growing louder and louder in the heart of the town.

'What's happening, Miss Molly?' one of the children whimpered. 'I'm scared.'

'I don't like it,' the youngest girl started to sob.

Molly glanced at the children. They all had the same expression etched upon their innocent faces. It was the confused look she recalled from her own youth during the bloody war. The look all sane folks have when trying to fathom the insanity of deadly conflict. Her heart was beating so hard, she was breathless as she clung to the door.

'Don't worry, children,' she managed to say in a vain bid to calm down her charges. 'Someone's just shooting their guns in the air, that's all.'

'I can hear crying, Miss,' the eldest of the boys said. 'How come women are crying?'

'I'm sure you're wrong, Johnny,' Molly frowned. 'Let's try not to upset the little ones.'

She turned back and squinted into the blazing

sunshine and licked her dry lips. Her attempted explanation had not settled the nervous youngsters down as she had hoped. They could hear the pathetic cries of females mixed into the cocktail of firing guns.

Even with their lack of maturity, the children instinctively sensed the danger that was gradually getting closer to their pitiful sanctuary.

Molly rested her temple against the door and pounded her small fist against the wooden wall. In her heart she knew that she had drawn the raiders to Rattlesnake Valley. Corbin had trailed her here just as he had done so many times before when she had been younger. To her father, she was simply a possession he refused to allow to escape his evil shadow.

The shooting echoed around the interior of the school.

Since she had arrived in Rattlesnake, Molly had found happiness and fulfilment. She had mistakenly thought that her horrendous past was behind her but know she knew that it had returned to reclaim her.

She opened her eyes and rubbed away the tears that had started to gather and then saw the familiar shape of her father riding through the sunlight and mist toward the small school. Molly tried to swallow, but her throat had tightened as if there were a noose around it. Colt Corbin was unmistakable as he sat astride his tall horse.

Molly turned and looked at the oldest of the children.

'Get the class under their desks, Johnny,' she said. 'Make sure you all remain there.'

Johnny did as he was instructed.

Within seconds, every one of the pupils was crouching under their desks. Molly could see every one of their tearful eyes looking back at her. They wanted reassurance and she could not give them anything except the look of horror that masked her beauty.

'Good,' Molly turned back and stared through the narrow gap between the door and the wall. Corbin was coming and she knew all too well what that meant. Death always rode with her deranged father.

Her mind raced as it searched for a way out of this situation that might save the youngsters' lives. Whatever happened, Molly thought, she had to prevent her father and the men who rode with him from entering the school. If they entered the small structure, all of the pupils would suffer a fate which none of them deserved.

Molly had witnessed what they could and would do without a single hint of remorse. She could not allow that. Above all she simply could not let them enter.

To prevent Corbin and his depraved raiders, Molly knew that there was only one thing she could do and that was to distract them. She would have to make the ultimate sacrifice.

Molly inhaled and straightened up.

'Don't any of you move until your parents get here,' she told the children. 'Just stay quiet and say your prayers and don't any of you come out. Stay put.'

The smallest of the children piped up, 'Where are you going, Miss Molly?'

Molly did not answer. She pulled the door just wide enough to allow her slim figure to slip out into the sunshine. She closed the door behind her and then moved to the edge of the small porch.

She defiantly looked at the approaching horse-man.

FOUR

The sound of gunshots drifted on the warm morning air and floated through the countless trees that loomed above the small settlement. The muscular horseman drew back on his long leathers and looked all around his mount and pack horses in a vain attempt to locate the origin of the distinctive gunshots.

The young hunter lifted one of his canteens and unscrewed its stopper as the faint noises of shooting continued to drift through the dense woodland.

The forested hills made it impossible to tell where the shooting was coming from and that troubled the youthful hunter, who had long considered himself the last of his breed.

He lifted the canteen and took a welcome drink and then lowered the container back until it sat on his saddle horn. He began screwing the stopper back on to the canvas container thoughtfully.

'I sure hope there ain't no other mountain men in these hills,' he remarked as he hung the canteen back on the saddle horn and checked some of his vast arsenal. 'I'd sure hate to arrive back at Rattlesnake with all this game and find that the townsfolk has already bought their meat and furs from some other varmint.'

Lane Chandler shook his head and tapped his boots against the sides of his powerful mount and continued to steer the animal between the trees. With every step his horse took on the precarious descent, Chandler could hear more shooting.

He looked in every direction and held his reins tightly in his massive hands. He shook his head thoughtfully.

'Who in tarnation is doing all that shooting?' he mumbled.

FIVE

The defiant girl stared across the schoolyard to the picket fence and the unmistakable figure of her father as he guided his mount toward it. Molly rested her knuckles on her hips and attempted to summon every last ounce of courage as she stepped down from the porch. The sun was warm and getting increasingly warmer with every passing second as Corbin started to slow down his mount. Even though she was shaking, the alert Molly suddenly noticed the other horse that her unpredictable father was leading.

Another saddle horse.

It was obvious why Corbin had brought that along, she reasoned. Just as she had feared, he intended that she go along with him and his raiders. As always, he refused to allow her to stray too far from his shadow.

45

Molly was terrified that he or his men might venture into the school and discover the children inside. Yet for all her fears, she managed to put on a convincing air of bravery as she slowly approached the man she loved and hated in equal portions.

His cruel eyes stared through the cigar smoke at her. It was not the look of a proud parent but more akin to that of a man with incestuous thoughts.

'Don't you look all fancy in that prissy dress, Molly?' he growled down at the girl who had fearlessly squared up to him. 'Look at you. Standing there all buttoned up to your neck and enough petticoats to hide your feet. You look like a real school ma'am.'

'That's because I am,' she snorted.

'No you ain't, girl,' Corbin argued. 'You're just a snot-nosed female who thinks she's better than her pa. It takes more than a fancy dress and a starched corset to do that. You're mine, Molly. Always have bin and always will be.'

Colt Corbin had always been able to strip his daughter of all her clothing and feelings of self-worth with a simple word.

It took every scrap of her inner strength not to burst into tears as she faced the merciless creature that she was unfortunate enough to have been sired by. She recalled the children inside the school house and stepped closer to the picket fence.

His sneering triggered memories that she had believed were long forgotten. Molly began to remember exactly why she had fled the abuse and torment to which Corbin had callously subjected her. She shuddered as graphic images flooded her mind. She clenched both her hands at her sides and stared at the rebel leader. One solitary notion kept her determined not to show the emotions that were drowning her in a mix of hostility and shame.

'So you found me,' Molly said as she watched her father holding his mount in check beside the white-washed picket fence. 'I knew you would.'

Corbin glared at her. There was no feeling in his cold eyes, only the satisfaction that he had managed to track down his most valuable possession. He exhaled a line of cigar smoke at the ground and then swung his leg over his saddle cantle and lowered himself to the ground.

'You can't hide from me, girl,' he hissed as he rounded his mount and untied the tethers of the spare saddle horse and led it toward the fence. 'I thought you knew that. Nobody ever gets away from me and my boys.'

Molly inhaled deeply and steadied her temper. The smell of gunsmoke drifted in the morning air from the heart of town as his motley band of men continued their savage rituals. She looked at Corbin. He seemed even taller than she remembered, and that unnerved her. She watched as he tied both horses' leathers to the fence without taking his dark eyes off her.

'Why d'you follow me?' she asked as she boldly started toward the merciless Corbin. 'It ain't out of fatherly love. You don't even know what that is, do you?'

'I give you love, girl,' he stated.

The statement sickened her. 'That was not love. That was the opposite of love and you damn well know it.'

Corbin pulled the cigar from his lips and tapped the ash before returning it to the corner of his mouth. He looked at her in a way that chilled the handsome female. It was not the look most fathers cast upon their children; it was something far darker.

'You got a big mouth just like your ma had,' he snarled as he curled a finger at her. 'Take these leathers and mount up before I whip your hide until its sweats blood, girl.'

Molly recalled how her mother had lived and died. She had then been forced to do things with Corbin that she knew were wrong. Anger swept through her rigid body as she opened the gate and stepped closer to the brutal man.

Corbin had used her in so many ways. She had been a human shield and a tempting diversion to those who saw her beauty and failed to notice his guns.

'Take the reins and get on that horse, girl,' he ordered in a deep growl. 'Your days of teaching school are over. I just give you your old job back.'

Not wanting the depraved Corbin to linger this close to the school house in case he heard the young female pupils and decided to satisfy his curiosity and other basic instincts, Molly accepted the reins and then looked at her long dress which was suitable for a school teacher but not exactly ideal attire to go riding in.

'I'll have to stop at the boarding house and change my clothes,' she told him as she indicated at the long dress. 'I can't ride in this.'

Corbin shook his head slowly and then suddenly grabbed her arm and pulled her toward him. He spat the cigar over her shoulder and then inhaled her perfume.

'Damn it all,' he grunted. 'You smell real sweet.'

'And you smell like a skunk,' she retorted.

Corbin tightened his grip on her wrists. She winced as pain raced through her petite form. He dragged her closer. Molly tried to fight but he was far too strong. He twisted her arm behind her and then forced her face first over the picket fence. The pointed slats of the fence dug into her middle as she vainly tried to fight him.

'Quit wrestling, Molly,' Corbin demanded before pressing his massive frame against her. 'You know what'll happen if you gets my sap rising.'

She stopped and raised an eyebrow.

'I told you,' she repeated. 'I've got to go to the boarding house and change into clothes more suitable for riding. This is my teaching clothes.'

A morbid grin etched Corbin's features as he loosened his grip and studied her dress. He had his daughter pinned over the picket fence. He began to nod and grunt as he pressed into her back to keep her subdued.

'Maybe your corset needs unlacing, girl?' he suggested. 'I'll loosen it for you.'

Molly suddenly felt her dress and petticoats being lifted and thrown over her shoulders. Then she saw the unmistakable shadow on the ground before her. He had drawn his sabre and was about to use its honed blade.

'What are you doing?' Molly asked fearfully.

His putrid breath answered as he continued to press down on her back. 'I'm gonna cut you free, Molly dear.'

She closed her eyes as she felt the broad bladed sword sever the laces in one expert manoeuvre. The corset fell at her feet. As Molly sighed in relief, she suddenly felt the razor sharp blade lingering around the base of her spine. One by one her petticoats began to follow the corset as Corbin peeled the bulky undergarments from her.

Molly closed her eyes. She silently prayed that he would stop when he reached her flesh. No matter how hard she wriggled though, she could not escape his over-powering determination.

Then as the last white petticoats slid down her thighs exposing her pale expanse of flesh, she heard the sound of horse's hoofs thundering toward the school.

Corbin released his vice-like grip and allowed her skirt to fall back over her naked skin as he took a step toward the horseman.

'What the hell do you want, Jango?' Corbin growled angrily at the rider.

Bodine pulled back on his reins and stopped his mount. His attention was not on his leader though, but rather on the shapely female standing on top of her ragged underwear.

Corbin grabbed the horse's bridle and glared up at Bodine as he returned the fearsome blade to its scabbard.

'I asked you a question, Jango,' he snarled.

Bodine looked into the fiery eyes of his leader and touched the brim of his hat. 'The boys are just about ready to leave this town, Colt. We got provisions and we killed every one of the horses that were scattered around town.'

Corbin rubbed his jaw as his cruel eyes watched his daughter mount the spare saddle horse. He returned his attention to Bodine.

'Did you find any money?' he asked.

'We sure did,' Bodine nodded excitedly as he studied the shapely female. 'I reckon we managed to get most of this town's cash.'

Corbin chuckled and then hoisted himself on top of his tall mount. He reached down and freed both horses' reins from the white picket fence. He turned his mount and watched as Molly duplicated his actions.

'I sure hope you didn't waste too much ammunition,' the depraved horseman snorted. 'I sure heard a hell of a lot of shooting.'

Bodine grinned, 'Some of them females were kinda ornery, Colt. They didn't hanker to being bedded. They took a little persuasion. We had to shoot a few of the more righteous ones.'

Corbin laughed and looked at his daughter. He reached across to touch her face. Molly shied away from his blood-stained hand.

'I got what I come here for,' he spat before pointing at the stern-faced female. 'Now let's get out of this town. Round up the rest of the boys.'

Bodine spurred back into the still choking gunsmoke as Corbin nodded at Molly.

'Remember, gal,' he warned. 'If you disobey me,

you'll get a dose of the same snake oil as the other womenfolk in this stinking town. Savvy?'

Molly nodded.

SIX

Few men cast a shadow as large as Lane Chandler. The young hunter was the last of his kind. He was a genuine mountain man who had learned his profession from his kinfolk but now plied his trade alone in the mountainous forests that surrounded the remote settlement of Rattlesnake Valley. His family were now buried around his small cabin perched on the mountainside overlooking the town for, as with most large people, their lifespan was far less than those who did less physical work.

The shots that Chandler had heard as he travelled back to Rattlesnake still echoed in his memory as he steered his mount and pack horses down the steep slope into brilliant and unforgiving sunshine. At first he had thought that it was hunters like himself but, as mile followed mile, he realized that there were no other hunters in this region any more.

Whatever he had heard was a mystery to the large rider draped in buckskin and furs. His keen eyes darted around the tranquil scene as his muscular mount began the steady descent toward the valley and the township.

The sun was big and merciless above the lone horseman as he guided his lathered-up mount and heavily-laden pack horses down the parched hillside toward the small settlement. The sturdy pack animals were burdened with the spoils of his latest hunt. The carcasses of two deer and numerous smaller animals were draped across the horses. Each securely tied down with woven leather ropes attached to the crude wooden frames, which rested upon the backs of the sturdy horses.

Although the township frowned on those they considered inferior to themselves like Chandler, they still had the taste for fresh game. The hunter knew that he would have no trouble in finding willing buyers for his perilous labours.

He pulled the battered brim of his hat to shield his eyes and eyed the small settlement he was closing in on with tired yet still alert eyes. Chandler repeatedly tapped his boots against the flanks of his mount. The tall black-tailed grey responded with its usual indifference and snorted its disapproval at the sun-bleached structures.

Chandler knew the horse was right in its contempt

for the snide two-faced people who purchased his wares and then ridiculed him. Towns were fine in small doses, but nothing could equal the thrill of the hunt. He regularly placed his life in danger and had to tend his own wounds when things went wrong. The hills were full of bears and, although he never hunted them, they had always posed a constant danger.

His own father had fallen victim to a large brown bear only three years earlier when they had been out hunting deer together. Chandler still bore the scars of the beast's long claws as he had vainly tried to save his father's life.

Townsfolk had no idea the true cost of providing fresh game for their tables. Chandler shrugged as the sure-footed horse continued on toward their goal.

Chandler wondered why so few men even considered hunting game for their meat and furs. It was the cheapest way to survive and feed a family in this dangerous territory but, for some reason he did not understand, they shunned the thought let alone the deed.

Hunting was ingrained into every fibre of his long muscular frame and yet that had always made him different. All his life he had been the outsider. Now his visits to Rattlesnake had been reduced to only when he was bringing them freshly killed game.

Civilization had always had a cruel streak.

Chandler did not understand it but had grown to accept it. Many men and women will cook meat provided by a butcher without a second thought of how it ended up hanging from the hooks in his shop, yet these same people will turn up their noses or simply mock a hunter who is daring enough to put his life on the line in order to try and provide food for themselves or others.

Chandler knew that when he hunted a deer, he had to track it and risk becoming the dinner of a more cunning mountain lion or territorial bear.

He was the last of his kind in these parts and regarded as someone who refused to accept the changing times and the benefits of conforming to what was acceptable. Chandler disregarded all attempts to change and liked being his own man even if the dangers outweighed the freedom it granted.

The shots he had heard in the deep forest returned to his tired mind. He glanced around at the grassland which his horses were walking through and then up at the town basking in the blistering sun.

Where had the shooting come from?

Who had been doing the shooting?

So many questions and not a single answer.

Rattlesnake appeared quiet as far as he could make out in the shimmering heat-haze. Chandler bit his lip as he encouraged his saddle horse to keep going.

As far as he knew, only the blacksmith Mort Riley and Sheriff Seth Brown had guns. If anyone else had guns, the hunter was unaware of it. He shook his head. Surely they would not be firing their weaponry off as though it were the fourth of July. They were far too old to get that worked up about anything, he sighed.

Then his mind drifted to the thought of beer. Cold beer.

That was the only thing that Rattlesnake had that Chandler figured was good about living in a town. He licked his cracked lips and started to nod to himself as he gripped his long leathers and encouraged the mount on toward the saloon.

A trail of dust rose up into the cloudless blue heavens as the single-minded horseman managed to get his horse to start cantering.

'When I get paid by the butcher I'm gonna drink that saloon dry, horse.' He laughed out loud and looked back at the following two pack horses. 'I'll then get me a bag of flour and some coffee beans and maybe a few horse biscuits for you pitiful critters.'

The horse increased its pace.

Lane Chandler screwed up his eyes and peered into the swirling heat-haze between the town and himself. It looked strangely quiet. The hunter glanced up at the cloudless heavens and then back at the weathered structures ahead.

'That's mighty odd,' he muttered. 'I can't see anyone, but it must be gone noon. I wonder where everybody is.'

Chandler encouraged the horses to increase their pace as curiosity started to get the better of him. He had never known Rattlesnake to have empty streets in the middle of the day before.

It troubled him.

As his mount trotted passed the school house, Chandler glanced longingly at the building. Yet it was not the wooden structure that he was thinking about, it was the beautiful female he knew only as Molly Drew who worked there.

Even though he had never had the courage to speak to her, he secretly longed for her. Ever since she had first arrived in Rattlesnake Valley, Chandler had been attracted to her unlike any of the other womenfolk in town.

To the hunter, she was different.

Yet men who live most of their lives alone have never found it easy to talk to women. Especially the beautiful ones.

As his mount headed deeper into the heart of the town, Chandler sadly scolded his feelings. 'She don't even know you exist, Lane. Forget such foolishness. No classy lady like her would want a dumb hunter to pay her any attention.'

Chandler realized that his words were probably correct. He had resolved himself to the fact that he would never find the companion he sought. The smell of death tended to linger on buckskin and few females liked the aroma.

His powerful hands eased back on his reins. The horse beneath him slowed to a mere walk. He exhaled heavily and returned his attention to the saloon, which he intended paying a visit once the town's butcher had paid him.

As the tall horse walked down the centre of the street, a thought occurred to Chandler. He lifted his heavy bulk off his saddle, turned and looked over the heads of his pack animals at the school.

'The school is kinda quiet for this time of day,' he said out loud and rubbed his unshaven jaw. 'I'd have figured the kids would be outside playing.'

He swung back around and stared at the buildings that flanked him. There was not a single soul walking along its boardwalks and that was troubling.

'Where are all the people?' he asked himself.

The skilled hunter glanced back at his pack animals and then looked again at the town he was riding through. Every store front was shuttered. His suspicions started to rise like the hair on the nape of his neck.

'This ain't right,' he muttered as his horse snorted and walked slowly down the long thoroughfare. 'This ain't right at all. Folks in Rattlesnake ain't no morning roosters, but they're usually up and walking around at this time. Where are they?'

None of the townsfolk were anywhere to be seen. Chandler raised himself up and balanced in his stirrups as he squinted at the façades to both sides of him. In all his days, he had never known Rattlesnake to be so barren of any living soul.

'Hell, even the hound dogs are gone,' he noticed.

The hunter's honed instincts sensed danger. Sometimes up in the wild forested hills, it was the difference between life and death. His backbone tingled like a divining rod under his shirt. Something in town just did not add up.

Chandler pushed his coat tails behind his holstered .45 and rested a large hand upon the horn of his saddle as he studied everything around his heavily-laden caravan. His eyes glanced down at the stock of his buffalo gun resting in its handmade scabbard.

Even though he was heavily armed, the hunter was starting to doubt the scene that surrounded him. It was eerily silent in Rattlesnake and that was something he had never experienced before. It troubled him.

Chandler bit his lip and swallowed hard.

He knew that he made a really large target. Beads of sweat rolled down his rugged features but it had

61

nothing to do with the blazing overhead sun. For the first time in a long while, he was nervous.

Men who risked their lives on an almost daily basis seldom gave a second thought to anything, but Chandler was now thinking about the quiet streets.

Where were the townsfolk?

He rubbed his cracked lips and nodded to himself.

'Quit fretting,' he told himself. 'All you need is a tall glass of beer. An ice-cold beer. Maybe it's a holiday and every one of the galoots in Rattlesnake is celebrating in the saloon.'

The young hunter straightened up and kicked the sides of his long-legged mount. He had almost convinced his doubting mind that weariness had clouded his thinking. There was nothing wrong. He was just dog-tired from weeks of hunting up in the perilous forest.

He shrugged as his mount gathered pace and rounded the corner into the main street. Even with the shimmering haze obscuring his view, Chandler knew exactly where the saloon was and steered his trusty mount toward it.

The rider smiled in anticipation of the money he would soon be paid for his wares. The cash would replenish his supplies and fill his belly with beer. Beer was the one thing he had yet to figure out how to make. His smile grew wider as he ran his fingers down his unshaven jaw.

'I should make a pretty penny today,' he noted as he looked back and checked the two horses trotting behind his wide shoulders. 'The folks of Rattlesnake will be throwing themselves at the critters I got here.'

The townsfolk liked the fact that Chandler was such an expert shot with any kind of weapon that you could barely find the wound. His trophies were usually killed with a solitary head shot so his regular customers did not have to laboriously dig buckshot out of its carcass.

Lane Chandler drew closer to his favourite building in the remote settlement. The unnamed saloon had a regular supply of the best beer brought into its unmarked boundaries twice a month. His grin grew wider and then faded from his grubby face as he passed the butcher's small store.

The hunter eased back on his long leathers and stared blankly at the shop. It was shuttered. His head tilted and studied the other buildings along the street.

They too were locked and shuttered.

Chandler rubbed his neck.

'That's odd,' he muttered before tapping his boots against the flanks of his saddle horse again. 'Maybe it is a holiday after all. I ain't never known the stores in this town to be closed up so early.'

The horse beneath his saddle continued along the street deeper into the heart of Rattlesnake. As its hoofs ate up the distance between the saloon and the stealthy horseman, Chandler suddenly felt his heart quicken its beating again.

No matter where he cast his keen eyes, he still did not see a living soul.

'What in hell is going on here?' he ranted angrily.

Suddenly a loud noise caused Chandler to haul rein and draw his six-shooter with incredible speed. His hand trembled as he glared into the sickening heat haze.

SEVEN

The hunter narrowed his stare as two massive black vultures erupted from the surrounding brush. They rose up through the undergrowth in all their terrifying glory sending debris showering over the startled Chandler. He steadied his mount as his heart slowly resumed beating. He gritted his teeth and slowly returned his gun to its holster. Drenched in the blinding light of the overhead sun, the town still looked quiet.

Too quiet.

Chandler raised himself and balanced in his stirrups as the grey continued on toward the saloon. He wondered what might happen if he were to start firing his .45 into the air. Would anyone venture out from their hiding places to take a look?

It seemed doubtful.

So far he had not seen anyone. What if they were all dead?

The notion seemed outrageous, but Chandler was running out of plausible options. A cold chill defied the blistering temperature and swept over the horseman. Chandler studied the dusty streets ahead. He was used to there being no onlookers watching his arrival. Folks in Rattlesnake Valley had never paid him any heed. He was just the young hunter who arrived in town every month or so with his animals laden with game. He recalled how the elderly sheriff had taunted him many times that he could earn far more money if he hunted wanted men instead of animals.

Yet Chandler had no stomach for fighting men, let alone killing them, even though it was far more profitable than risking his hide hunting in hills full of mountain lions and grizzly bears.

Hidden beneath its porch overhang and bathed in the blackest of shadows, the saloon caught his eagle-eyed attention. He squinted hard at the usually noisy and busy building.

To his total disbelief, it looked as quiet as the rest of the structures he had passed.

'That can't be,' he drawled as his mount got closer to the normally busy saloon.

Yet the saloon appeared to be locked up just like all the other buildings in Rattlesnake Valley. He felt the sweat rolling down his back under the merciless rays of the sun. He sighed heavily as he guided his mount toward the locked up drinking hole.

'Damn it's hot,' he sighed as he once again lowered himself back on to his saddle. 'I ain't never known it so hot before and by the look of that saloon I'm gonna have to drink out of the trough to cool down.'

Chandler pushed the brim of his hat back until it rested on the crown of his dark brown hair. The thought of beer filled his mind.

'Maybe the doors just shut.' He tried to settle his nerves as the tall grey trotted. 'It don't mean the saloon's locked up just coz the door's closed.'

As his mount cantered, Chandler looked to both sides of the street in a vain search for life. Yet no matter how hard his eyes strained, Chandler still saw no one.

He shook his head. Beads of sweat floated in the sunlight like diamonds falling from the sky. The gentle giant slowed the grey to a walk.

Still expecting the citizens of Rattlesnake to suddenly appear, Chandler twisted and turned on his saddle in a vain search for them. His eyes darted to every corner of the street but there was not a single man, woman or child to be seen. He exhaled heavily.

His mind raced as his horse headed straight toward the saloon. Yet even before he reached the wooden structure, his eyes noted that its doors were shuttered and locked.

Chandler stared at the padlock on the double doors and silently cursed. He reined in and stopped the grey just beside the water trough. He dismounted in one fluid action and held the grey's bridle before allowing the animal to drop its head and start drinking. Chandler walked around the tail of his mount and carefully led the pack horses to the trough. Both heavily-burdened animals started to quench their thirst as the hunter rested his knuckles on his hips.

'Something's mighty wrong here,' he clenched his fists and patted his saddle horse. 'This is the first time I've seen this saloon shuttered in the middle of the day.'

None of his horses paid him any attention as Chandler strode across the white sand and stepped up on to the boardwalk. His eyes burned as they stared at the padlock. His large left hand reached out, grabbed the lock and shook it firmly.

The saloon was locked up tight.

By the look of it, the saloon had not opened up today.

He wondered why.

The large man walked back to his mount and then looked over his shoulder at the padlock before stepping back down on to the sand. Chandler knew that he had to get his game out of the brilliant sunlight soon. He rubbed his neck and looked around and noticed other closed store doors.

'This ain't good,' he muttered.

He was confused and more than a little troubled.

For what felt like an eternity, the muscular hunter tried to figure out what was happening in a town where nothing ever happened. Then he thought about the veteran lawman who always seemed to know everything.

'The sheriff will know what's going on,' Chandler turned on his heels and headed across the street toward the diminutive building where he knew he could locate the lawman. 'Seth Brown will have the answer. The sheriff knows everything in Rattlesnake.'

Chandler stepped up on to the boardwalk, reached out to the brass door handle and went to enter. His entire body bumped into the locked door. He rattled the handle but the door refused to open.

'Don't tell me old Seth has gone fishing,' the youngster sighed heavily and shrugged. He glanced back at the locked saloon and then cast his attention to the other stores along the street. Each of them had closed doors and he knew that every single one of them ought to be open for business. 'What in tarnation is going on here?'

Chandler moved to the window, rubbed its grubby pane and cupped the sides of his face with his hands. He pressed his nose against the glass and peered into the dark interior of the office. For a few moments he did not see anything. Then something caught his eye in its dark interior.

The young hunter squinted harder and then knew what it was he was looking at. An icy chill traced his spine. His eyes tightened as he strained to confirm his theory. He straightened up and rubbed the nape of his neck. Chandler was in no doubt what he could just make out from the window.

It was an outstretched leg.

EIGHT

The weathered door shattered and splintered into a million fragments as it succumbed to Chandler's sturdy shoulder. The hunter staggered to a halt as a cloud of dust and debris floated around the small office. Even before his eyes had adjusted to the dim interior, his nose caught the unmistakable scent of death.

He glanced down at the floor as his eyes adjusted to the dimness close to the window. A shudder of horror went through his large body as he slowly knelt beside the lifeless body of Sheriff Brown.

Chandler was no stranger to the sight of death, but not like this. He swallowed and cleared his throat as his large hands checked the lawman. As he moved the limp body on to its side, he saw the blood.

So much blood.

It was already starting to congeal around the

ancient lawman's body as Chandler pressed his fingers against the neck of the dead man. Just as he had anticipated, there was no pulse.

'Damn it all, Seth,' he exhaled. 'What you wanna go getting yourself killed for?'

The hunter checked the lawman's chest until his fingers found the tear in the shirt. He eased the body on to its back and pealed the shirt away from the hideous chest wound.

Brown had been skewered with a knife, he concluded. A big knife. Its blade had penetrated the old man's heart and instantly sent the sheriff off to meet his ancestors. The hunter had never seen a man stuck like a pig before and did not care for the sight.

Chandler shook his head and then rose back up to his full height. A torrent of thoughts flowed through his mind as he stared down at the elderly sheriff.

Who had done this?

Why had someone killed the old lawman?

No matter how hard he tried, Chandler could not come up with any answers. There was no one in Rattlesnake capable of this sort of outrage.

Or was there?

The hunter moved back out on to the weathered boardwalk and rubbed his neck with his massive hand as his eyes darted around the deserted street. Chandler pushed his coat tails over the grip of his holstered six-shooters and rested the palms of his hands upon their wooden grips. A strange dread washed over him as he became aware that for the first time in his life he might have to use his arsenal of weaponry on a two-legged animal.

It was a thought he did not savour. Killing critters was one thing, but whoever had stabbed Sheriff Brown was a breed of *hombre* he had never encountered before.

What had he ridden into?

Chandler stepped down on to the sandy street and crossed back to his three horses. His tall grey was still drinking its fill as he moved to where his various hunting rifles hung from the saddle.

He inhaled deeply. His barrel chest expanded as he continued to search every inch of the street. Whoever had killed Brown might still be in Rattlesnake Valley, he told himself as he rested a hand on one of his holstered guns.

The killer of the sheriff could be hiding anywhere in the sprawling settlement watching him. The notion chilled the hunter. Again, he felt like a target.

He rubbed his teeth with his bare knuckle.

'If somebody's hiding out in town they could pick me off real easy,' he mumbled. 'Maybe that's what's happened to the rest of the folks in town.'

As the words left his cracked lips, the burly figure pulled his long leathers free of the hitching rail. The black-tailed grey raised its head and snorted as

Chandler led it away from the trough with the pack animals in tow.

Flanked by his animals, Chandler walked down the middle of the street toward the livery stable set at the very end of town. As he plodded along, he listened out for any sound that might mean he was being observed.

Yet Rattlesnake Valley remained as quiet as a grave-yard.

He reached the large structure and entered through its wide open doors. The interior of the livery was a lot cooler than the sun-baked street. The well-built hunter reached the heart of the building.

Chandler stopped.

He noticed that the coals in the forge were grey. Its fire had long since died. Chandler knew that no blacksmith worth his salt would ever allow his forge to extinguish deliberately.

The hunter caught an aroma that he recognized.

It was the scent of death.

NINE

All livery stables had a familiar fragrance, but it was another scent that filled his flared nostrils and alerted his honed instincts. It was the familiar smell only the dying can create as they succumb to death. Chandler released his grip on the reins and slowly turned toward the darkest section of the livery.

He did not move an inch from where he had stopped.

His eyes scanned the black corner.

It did not take long to spot the slaughtered horses in their stalls around the back wall of the large structure. Chandler frowned in horror at the sight and smell of the dead horses. It seemed obvious to the hunter that whoever had killed Sheriff Brown had also killed every single horse in the livery.

'Somebody didn't want to be trailed,' he concluded.

Then he saw something else in the far corner. He placed his hand on one of his gun grips and strode across the sod floor toward the origin of the smell. Then he heard the flies. Far more flies than usual were buzzing frantically in the darkness. Only death drew this amount of flies, he reasoned.

Chandler stopped and lowered his head.

The sight of the blacksmith crumpled in the corner was like a kick to his guts. He swallowed hard and shook his head as he continued his approach. As the gentle giant passed the stalls, he noticed that every horse within the livery had suffered the same fate as the blacksmith. They lay in pools of their own scarlet blood.

It was horrendous to see so many dead horses, but Chandler continued on toward the equally sickening vision of the blood-covered body in the corner.

His eyes surveyed the body as he towered above it. His natural instinct was to speak to the blacksmith, but Chandler knew that was pointless.

The blacksmith would never have another conversation with anyone apart from the angels, he thought. Chandler defied his own revulsion and stooped over the dead man. Even though the blacksmith was roughly the same size and build as Chandler, the young hunter effortlessly plucked him off the ground and cradled him in his arms. The flies followed Chandler out into the blazing sunshine as the hunter carried the lifeless corpse away from the stable.

An unfamiliar rage started to fester in the guts of the hunter as he carefully carried his friend down the middle of the empty street.

The dead man was heavy, but Chandler did not seem to notice the weight as he strode through the blistering sun. He headed for the funeral parlour on the corner and stepped up on to the boardwalk. He moved passed its impressive window with its gold lettering to the parlour's locked door. His boot kicked at the door a few times.

'You in there, Cecil?' he shouted. 'Open up.'

There was no reply to either his question or demand. He gritted his teeth and then kicked the door with such anger that its frame broke free. The door swung inward and Chandler trailed it.

Chandler moved to a counter and laid the lifeless body on top of it. The hunter sighed heavily as he saw the horrific wound clearly for the first time.

'They gutted you like a fish, Mort,' he said angrily.

The knife wound was similar to the one that had killed Sheriff Brown. The savagery staggered Chandler. He could not imagine how anyone could do that to another man.

Chandler bit his lip and sighed heavily.

'What in tarnation is going on here?' he growled as he rested his hands on the counter beside the body. 'None of this makes any sense. No sense at all. Why'd anyone wanna kill Mort and Seth? They never had any money.'

He eased his massive bulk around and looked out through the busted doorway. The sun made the street appear almost white for a few seconds as the hunter moved back toward it.

'Is that you, Lane?' the shaking voice startled the young man. With an agility that defied his bulk, Chandler swung around and drew one of his guns as though he were being crept up on by a wild beast. His eyes tightened as they searched for the owner of the voice.

'Show yourself or I'll start shooting,' Chandler hissed as his gun sought out the trembling voice. 'I ain't joshing. Show yourself.'

'Don't shoot,' Cecil Farmer squealed as he suddenly appeared from out of the parlour's back room with his hands raised. 'It's me.'

Chandler lowered his six-gun and then holstered it as he stared at the elderly undertaker moving sheepishly out from the back room and heading toward him.

A sense of total relief washed over the hunter as he sighed heavily and slowly released the hammer of his .45. He shook his head at his elderly friend.

'What the hell were you doing hiding back there, Cecil?' he asked as the smaller man lowered his arms and sat down on a hard-back chair. 'Why didn't you answer when I called out? I could have killed you.'

Farmer leaned back against the chair. A visible vein pulsated on his temple as the undertaker attempted to steady his shattered nerves. Sweat rolled from the top of his bald head and dripped off his jaw as he sat shaking. 'I didn't know who you were, Lane boy.'

Chandler moved closer. He had never seen Farmer so shaken before. 'Are you OK, Cecil? You look as sick as I feel.'

'I thought you were one of them,' the undertaker said as tears ran from his eyes and mixed with the sweat. 'I figured you had come back to finish off the folks you missed the first time.'

Chandler pushed his hat back until it rested on the crown of his head. He looked down at the demure old man and frowned at the sight. He had never seen anyone so visibly terrified before and it troubled the youngster.

'You seen them?' he asked.

Farmer looked at Chandler through his watery eyes. 'I didn't see any of them but I heard them, Lane. I heard what they were doing. I heard the screams of the townsfolk that they were doing it to. I've never heard men and women make those kind of noises before, Lane. Whatever them raiders were doing to them folks, it must have been monstrous.'

79

Horror filled the hunter. He patted the shoulder of the undertaker in a clumsy effort to comfort him.

'You mean the varmints that killed old Mort and Seth also killed women, Cecil?' he asked in disbelief.

'Most of the screams were female, Lane,' the undertaker confirmed. 'There ain't no mistaking women in terror and pain.'

Chandler could hardly believe what he was being told. The hunter had no real experience of what evil men could and would do to innocents. He seldom mixed with anyone except when he was delivering his monthly catch in Rattlesnake. The forest was his world and even the most dangerous of animals never unleashed the sort of savagery that Rattlesnake had just endured.

Only men were driven by the poisonous mixture of greed, lust and pure evil. Chandler was just beginning to learn this and it chilled the young hunter to the bone.

'Are you sure that some of them females were killed, Cecil?' Chandler asked anxiously.

'It sure sounded like they was being killed, Lane,' the undertaker gave a nod of his head. 'Them bastards killed a hell of a lot of folks, boy. I'd hate to guess how many.'

'I ain't seen any dead or wounded womenfolk, Cecil.' Chandler rubbed the sweat from his face and looked back at the street. He was confused and more than a little troubled by the horrifying information he had just received. He was angry and getting angrier with every beat of his heart. Chandler was a hunter, but could not understand anyone who killed people, especially the female variety.

'They must have dragged their bodies off and hid them so nobody passing through would know what had happened.' The undertaker reasoned.

Chandler nodded in agreement and then gestured at the body of the blacksmith laid across the funeral parlour counter.

'I found Mort inside his livery, Cecil,' Chandler stated as he tried to work out what was going on in Rattlesnake. 'All the horses there were dead as well. The livery's a damn blood bath. Every one of them had been stabbed just like Mort.'

Cecil Farmer glanced up at the big man. 'They killed the horses as well? Why'd they wanna do that for, Lane?'

Finally a question he had an answer for, Chandler thought as he leaned over the undertaker. The young mountain man tilted his head.

'So they couldn't be trailed,' Chandler reasoned. 'That's the only reason I can figure. They figured that there wouldn't be another horse in Rattlesnake until the next stagecoach arrives. They had no way of knowing that I was headed here from up in the hills.'

Farmer nodded in agreement, 'Yeah. That makes

a lot of sense. They sure didn't want anyone round-ing up a posse and following them.'

'Who are "they", Cecil?' Chandler wondered.

Farmer sighed heavily and rubbed his aching chest. His heart was still pounding like a war drum beneath his finery. Chandler leaned over the under-taker thoughtfully.

'Who were they, Cecil?' he repeated. 'Who in tar-nation is this bunch of loco-beans exactly?'

'I'm not sure, Lane boy,' the older man sighed heavily and dried his face with a handkerchief. 'They rode into town just after sunrise and then started slaughtering folks. They were using knives at first so nobody would know what was up. Then they started to use their guns. I can still hear them damn guns, boy. I was so scared I locked the office door and hid out back in one of my coffins.'

Chandler moved to the door and looked around the locked-up buildings in a vain attempt to see someone. There was no sign of life anywhere in Rattlesnake Valley. If there were bodies, he sure could not see any. He turned his head and glanced over his shoulder at Farmer.

'They couldn't have killed everyone,' he muttered.

Farmer shrugged, 'I'm betting a lot of folks just locked their doors and hid when they realized what was happening, Lane. I'll bet they're still hiding. I only showed my face 'coz I recognized your voice.'

Chandler shook his head slowly in utter disbelief.

'The townsfolk must be mighty scared and no mistake,' he said through gritted teeth. 'I don't get it. Rattlesnake ain't got nothing worth killing for.'

Farmer's expression suddenly altered as his elderly brain began to put two and two together. He straightened up on the wooden chair.

'I just had me a notion, Lane,' he blurted. 'I reckon I might have just worked out who this bunch is and what they came here for.'

Chandler raised his eyebrow as he wondered why the townsfolk did not put up more of a fight, 'Ain't none of the folks in town got any guns, Cecil?'

The ancient undertaker squinted against the bright sunlight that was reflecting off the water trough outside the parlour.

'The sheriff and Mort here had guns,' he stated. 'They didn't do them much good though, did they? I don't reckon there can be more than five guns in the rest of Rattlesnake. It's been a long time since we needed guns.'

'Hell,' Chandler interrupted. 'I got more than that hanging off my black-tailed grey, Cecil. Plus I got me this pair of six-shooters strapped to my hips.'

Farmer sighed heavily, 'Up until now nobody in Rattlesnake figured they needed guns. Seth only wore his six-gun when he remembered to put his gun-belt on. You're a hunter and need your weaponry up in them hills, but the rest of us ain't.'

The large figure rubbed his neck as his mind tried to get around the information it was absorbing. 'I just don't understand what them *hombres* wanted here, Cecil. Hell, Rattlesnake Valley ain't even got a bank.'

The older man suddenly remembered what he had worked out a few moments before. He looked at the young hunter, stood up and moved to the side of the troubled Chandler. Farmer placed a shaking hand on the arm of the youngster and got his full attention.

'Molly Drew,' he said the name drily.

TEN

Chandler stared blankly at the undertaker beside him. He could not understand why the undertaker had just uttered the name of the school teacher.

'What's this gotta do with Molly?' he asked.

Farmer looked straight into the eyes of the younger man. 'It's just a notion, but I got me a feeling that this is all about young Molly, Lane.'

The startling statement caught the hunter by surprise.

Chandler raised his eyebrows in bewilderment and looked long and hard at the undertaker.

'What about Molly?' he asked. 'She's just a young gal who teaches school. Why would a gang of insane killers come here and start killing because of her? That don't make any sense. No sense at all.'

Farmer moved even closer.

'It makes perfect sense, Lane,' he argued.

'Explain, Cecil.' Chandler had been smitten with Molly ever since he had first set eyes upon her. The thought that she could be to blame for this outrage did not sit well with him. 'Explain how Molly could have anything to do with any of this.'

'Calm down, Lane,' Farmer urged his younger companion as he could see the confusion in Chandler's face. 'I don't mean she had anything to do with this, but she's the reason these senseless killers came here.'

'Keep talking, Cecil,' Chandler said bluntly. 'Tell me exactly what you mean. I get kinda ornery when innocent gals get blamed for things they couldn't possibly know anything about.'

'You don't understand.'

'Then make me understand, Cecil.'

The undertaker suddenly realized that apart from the dead sheriff, he was the only man in town who knew the truth about the pretty school teacher. He had to try and explain to Chandler.

'Listen up, Lane. Molly Drew ain't her real name,' he began. 'The sheriff was ordered by a couple of secret service hombres not to reveal her true identity to anyone because she's under government protection. Seth confided in me because he wanted somebody else to know who she really is.'

Chandler could not believe what he was hearing.

'It sounds a bit far-fetched, Cecil,' he said.

'I swear it's all true, Lane boy,' Farmer insisted as he gripped Chandler's muscular arm tightly. 'Seth was scared and by the looks of it, he was right to be scared.'

The hunter thought about the bloody situation and shrugged, 'I reckon you're right, Cecil. Keep talking, I'm listening.'

'Molly's real name ain't Drew,' Farmer continued. 'It's Corbin. Molly Corbin. She's really the daughter of Colt Corbin the rebel outlaw. That gal suffered a heap of abuse and the secret service put her here for her own safety. I don't know how, but somehow Corbin learned that she was here. Him and his bunch of killers come looking for her this morning and I'll bet every cent I've got, they found her.'

Lane Chandler's face went ashen. It was as though every drop of colour had been drained from his flesh as the old timer's words sank into his weary mind.

He shook his head and stared blankly at the floor-boards inside the funeral parlour. 'Colt Corbin is her father?'

'Yep,' Farmer nodded. 'Seth told me what them secret service *hombres* told him about Corbin. That bastard is evil, Lane. That young filly has suffered. All she wanted was a chance to escape and build herself a new life.'

Chandler gulped as he remembered the torrid tales of the atrocities the Confederate rebel and his cohorts were credited with. To them the war had never ended. There was a certain breed of men who refused to admit defeat and renounce the sickening skills war had taught them. Corbin and his raiders were said to be such a breed of men who had never surrendered, like so many of their fellow Confederates.

The hunter rubbed the sweat off his face with his large hands and shook with anger. 'Why would they kill innocent folks if all they wanted was Molly?'

'Because they can, son,' Farmer said softly. 'That kind of vermin do anything they wanna do until somebody stops them.'

Chandler looked down on the undertaker.

'I don't understand,' he naively said.

'You're too young to remember the war, Lane,' Farmer sighed as his mind recalled the horror he had lived through. 'War brings out the worst in folks. Some critters get a taste for killing and just can't quit. They kill for the sheer joy of it, boy.'

Chandler stared hard at the undertaker.

'They kill folks just coz they like it?'

'Yep,' Farmer nodded. 'They kill and do a lot of worse things as well.'

Suddenly a panic swept through every sinew in the large hunter's body as he began to understand what Farmer meant. He tried to swallow, but there was no spittle.

'You reckon they took Molly?' he stammered. 'Why would they take her, Cecil? They ain't thinking of killing her, are they?'

Cecil shook his head, 'Corbin ain't thinking of killing her, Lane. What him and his gang are intending is probably far worse.'

Chandler glared down at the undertaker, 'Are you telling me that Corbin might have come to Rattlesnake to get his daughter?'

Farmer slowly nodded. 'I believe so, Lane.'

The large man struggled with the notion that one of the most notorious killers to have come out of the war had been in the quiet settlement. He glanced at the undertaker as he slowly made his way out on to the boardwalk and rested his wide back against one of its uprights. He bit his lower lip as he began to think about the attractive girl he had known as Molly Drew.

It seemed impossible that she could possibly be related to anyone like Colt Corbin, but he trusted the word of the old undertaker and knew it must be the truth.

The thought of the beautiful Molly filled his mind. He had wanted to sweet talk her for more than a year, but had never been able to muster the courage. He was always tongue-tied when faced by the school teacher. He had never managed to utter a single word when in her company. Like most burly men,

Chandler was awkward when faced with an attractive member of the opposite sex.

His father had taught him how to survive by hunting, but that was where his education had ended. He rubbed his damp neck with his massive palm as the smaller man joined him on the porch. Farmer sat down on the window sill and stared up at the young hunter. He had been around long enough to recognize the ailment that Chandler was suffering from.

'You liked little Molly, huh?' the undertaker asked.

Chandler turned his face away from the wiser and older man as he felt his cheeks redden.

'I reckon so,' he answered bashfully.

'How come you never told her?' Farmer pressed as he found his pipe and withdrew it from his vest pocket.

Chandler glanced back at the older man. 'You know why.'

Farmer struck a match and held its flame above his pipe and inhaled smoke until he was confident that the tobacco was lit. The undertaker tossed the match at the sand.

'Nope, I don't know why,' he said through a cloud of smoke as he eyed the only true man he had ever encountered in Rattlesnake Valley. 'Tell me, Lane. How come you didn't tell that gal how you felt?'

Chandler turned and looked hard at the old man.

'Molly wouldn't care to be soft spoken to by some-thing like me, Cecil. She'd have either screamed or laughed. I ain't never bin able to figure which would be worse.'

'Molly is a kind girl,' Farmer insisted. 'That gal would never do either to you. She likes you.'

The tall hunter paced to where the undertaker was perched and looked down at him. 'How'd you know she likes me, Cecil?'

Farmer smiled and pulled the stem from his lips. He pointed his pipe at the hunter.

'She told me so,' he replied. 'That gal has a twinkle in her eyes every time some galoot mentions your name. Molly likes you a lot, Lane. I reckon she likes you better than any of the other guys in Rattlesnake. All she needs is an excuse to let you know.'

Chandler shook his head in disbelief, 'A gal like her wouldn't give me a second glance. You're making it up.'

'I ain't,' Farmer sighed as he placed the stem of his pipe back in his mouth and gripped it with his teeth. 'I once had a female who looked at me the way she looks at you, boy. I never had the guts to talk to her either and she up and got hitched to a riverboat gambler. Don't make the same mistake that I made. You'll regret it for the rest of your days if you do.'

Chandler swung around on his heels and stared at

the silent street. He punched his fists together and pulled his hat brim down to shade his eyes.

'Do you reckon Molly is still in town, Cecil?' he asked nervously. 'For all we know she's hiding like everybody else.'

'You're right, Lane,' Farmer stood and stepped beside his young friend. 'I'll go start looking for her. I might have bin wrong about her father and his boys doing all the killing. It might have bin another bunch of loco cowboys.'

Chandler nodded, 'You check every store and house. If you find her, yell your guts out.'

Farmer stepped down into the sunlight, 'What are you gonna do while I'm looking for Molly?'

Chandler pointed at the tall wooden livery stable and then nodded firmly. 'I'm gonna head back to the livery and check the area out carefully, Cecil.'

'What for, boy?' The undertaker tilted his head back and watched the hunter stride back to where he had discovered the blacksmith and the dead horses.

Chandler rested his hands on his holstered guns. 'You forget, Cecil. I'm a hunter and if anyone can figure out who and what done all this killing, it's me.'

Farmer nodded and then raced as fast as his legs could carry him to the very edge of town to start his search for Molly Drew. The elderly undertaker wondered if it might not be better for Molly if she were also dead like the blacksmith. At least Mort Riley's pain had ended.

Who knew what fate awaited the young woman?

ELEVEN

The intrepid search for the beautiful young Molly Drew had been a fruitless effort for both Farmer and Chandler. All either man had discovered were frightened townsfolk huddled in the darkest of corners all around Rattlesnake Valley. Yet the terrified inhabitants of the small town were the lucky ones. Both the hunter and the undertaker had also found the bodies of both men and women.

The near-naked females had been killed after Corbin's raiders had abused them in a manner neither Chandler nor the far older Farmer had ever imagined possible. The undertaker had thought that he had witnessed the worst atrocities possible during the brutal conflict years earlier, but he had been wrong.

What the raiders had done to the town's women was far worse than anything the old man had seen during the war. The bodies of a handful of men had also been discovered by both Farmer and Chandler. They had died trying to defend the helpless females from a fate that had proven to be far worse than their ultimate deaths.

Chandler had no knowledge of the barbaric things that he too had found. He knew what wild animals could do to the unprepared who dared to enter the wilderness, but he had never seen anything like the savage carnage that had happened in Rattlesnake.

Even after being told that the raiders had departed the remote town, the streets were virtually empty. The survivors were in shock and still petrified.

Chandler's buckskins were stained with so much blood that they were no longer brown. They were a deathly shade of crimson. The muscular youth had carried each and every one of the bodies and carefully placed them in the yard behind the funeral parlour as Cecil Farmer had instructed him.

As he lay the last of the stricken corpses down on the ground and straightened up, he saw Farmer walking through the parlour toward him.

The look of disbelief was carved into the old man's face.

Farmer paused beside the rear door and watched silently as Chandler moved toward him. Even though they looked at one another, neither spoke.

The undertaker trailed Chandler through the

back room and into the front of the funeral parlour where the body of the blacksmith still lay on the counter.

Farmer opened an office drawer, pulled out a bottle of whiskey and silently offered it to Chandler. The young hunter gave a nod of his head and accepted the fiery liquor gratefully.

The undertaker was seeing Chandler in a new light. The hunter had proven himself during the previous hour.

As Chandler pulled its cork with his teeth, Farmer found a pair of tin cups and shook the dust from them. He held both vessels out as the hunter filled them with the amber liquor.

They drank without uttering a word and stared out into the sun-baked street. They had not found the woman that Rattlesnake knew as Molly Drew, but they had discovered her undergarments close to the fence that surrounded the school.

Farmer feared the worst, but could not tell his young friend what he believed to be the young woman's fate. He knew that Chandler was love-struck and angry with himself for not conveying his feelings to Molly.

Now both men were afraid that it was probably too late.

Farmer filled their cups again and stared at Chandler as he sipped his whiskey. He had never really spoken to the hunter before and felt guilty about that. The young hunter was quiet yet a kind soul at heart.

He was probably the most honest man that the veteran undertaker had ever met during his long life. Farmer glanced over the top of his cup at his friend.

'You did good, Lane,' he said respectfully. 'I could never have managed to get all those bodies back here on my lonesome. Thanks.'

Chandler nodded and kept staring at the street.

'I can't stop thinking about Molly, Cecil,' he admitted before taking a mouthful of the strong liquor and swallowing.

'Me too, boy,' Farmer said. 'But what can we do?'

Chandler looked at the undertaker, 'You can't do nothing but I can, old timer.'

'What you mean, Lane?' Farmer wondered what the young hunter meant. 'You got something brewing in that young head of yours?'

Chandler nodded.

'By all accounts, according to most of the survivors I talked to, there are seven or eight raiders with Corbin,' Farmer mentioned the fact fearfully. 'That's way too many for anyone to tackle single-handed, Lane.'

The younger man finished his whiskey and placed the cup on to the counter before turning to look at his friend. He ran his fingers through his mane of unkempt hair and then replaced his hat.

'They've got Molly, Cecil,' Chandler drawled as he walked to the porch. 'I intend getting her back even if it costs me my life. I don't intend letting them hombres do to her what they done to the females out back.'

'I'll go with you,' Farmer heard himself say. 'I might be old but I ain't dead yet.'

'You ain't coming along with me,' Chandler shook his head and stepped out into the sun. 'You got a lot of work to tend to here, old timer. I might not be a hardened killer like them critters who got Molly, but I am a hunter and I know them hills yonder.'

Farmer felt his legs ache as he followed his friend and knew that Chandler was right. He managed to reach the boardwalk as the large youngster stepped down into the street.

'They're savage killers, boy,' Farmer vainly pleaded. 'You ain't a killer.'

Chandler glanced over his shoulder.

'If that's what it takes to save Molly, then that's what I'll become, Cecil.' He touched his hat brim and then continued on to the livery.

The undertaker was not convinced that his young friend could turn his incredible marksmanship on to Corbin and his equally deadly cohorts. 'Killing folks is a whole lot different to hunting and trapping animals, Lane. Do you really think you can do this?'

'Sure I can,' Chandler paused in the middle of the street and stared at Farmer. Neither were convinced by the statement, but both hoped that the hunter would not end up like the bodies out back of the funeral parlour. 'I'm gonna get my horse and track them damn varmints before they reach the range. They don't know them hills like I do. Once I catch up with them, I'll get Molly back.'

'You make it sound real simple, Lane.'

Chandler just smiled.

Farmer rested his bony knuckles on his hips and shook his head forlornly. He knew that nothing could change the mind of his lovesick friend.

'You're going to risk your neck for Molly?' he asked.

Chandler nodded, turned and carried on walking toward the livery stable. The muscular youth raised his voice. 'If I don't come back, you can tell the butcher that he don't have to pay me for the game I left in the livery.'

Cecil Farmer rubbed his neck thoughtfully before turning and heading back toward his parlour. As he stepped on to the boardwalk, he shouted through the shimmering haze.

'You'd better come back, boy' he wheezed. 'I ain't digging all them graves on my lonesome.'

TWELVE

The high-shouldered grey stallion moved swiftly through the forested hills as Chandler used every scrap of his hunting skill to catch up with his elusive prey. For the first time in his life, Chandler had turned his abilities on the vicious men who had snatched Molly and slain so many of the residents of Rattlesnake. The hunter had read the hoof tracks well and had calculated the route Corbin and the raiders were taking. They were heading toward the fast-flowing river and following its course until they reach the open range.

Chandler knew instinctively which trail he had to ride in order to overtake Corbin and his blood-thirsty followers. The black-tailed grey climbed the slippery hillside with the agility of a mountain goat. The trees were so dense that their foliage masked everything ahead of the horseman. Chandler knew that it would be close to sundown before he caught up with the merciless band, but the image of Molly kept him forcing the grey onward.

Neither the horseman nor his trusty mount would have chosen this trail if it were not for the fact that it was imperative to catch up with the raiders.

Chandler knew that Molly had been taken by force. As the sturdy horse cleared the steep incline and rested on top of a rugged outcrop of boulders, the hunter surveyed the rugged mountainside below him.

As he squinted down through the countless branches, he caught sight of the river. White flashes of sunlight reflected back up at him. Chandler then leaned forward and listened for any unusual sound.

The hunter knew only too well that when men entered the wilderness, even the birds fell silent. Men who were unfamiliar with this terrain would be the only living creatures to make a noise.

Chandler had been taught from an early age to be as silent as he could when hunting. Every living thing in the forested hills used their hearing more than their eyesight so they could tell when danger was close. Chandler continued to look down through the trees and boulders.

Then he heard them.

None of their horses had been trained to be silent as they moved through the untamed terrain, unlike his trusty black-tailed grey. Chandler could hear the horses' hoofs as well as the mumbling of riders, even though it was impossible to see them. He looked to where he knew the river was headed and turned his mount. He had to get downwind of them so they would not catch his scent. Even though it was doubtful that Corbin or any of his men would be able to catch his scent as he grew closer to them, Chandler knew that their horses would get alarmed when they did. Horses were skittish animals with senses far more sensitive than most animals.

Chandler was well aware that if the rebels' horses caught even a mere whiff of either his horse or himself, they would start to panic.

The grey stallion carefully moved across the high ridge as it slowly made its way down to river level. The highly-trained horse quietly moved between the trees and boulders as its master continued looking down to the river below his high vantage point.

Chandler had no idea what he would do when faced with the brutal murderers who had ripped the heart out of Rattlesnake and taken Molly hostage.

All he knew was that he was going to try and rescue her, even if it cost him his life. As he stared upward through the tree canopies, he noticed that the sky was slowly darkening.

He held on to his long leathers and allowed the agile mount to find its own course down through the precarious trail toward the fast-moving river.

With every step of the long-legged grey, the sound of the horsemen far below grew louder. They were totally unaware that they were being hunted.

The hunter was closing the distance between them and himself. Chandler was scared. For the first time in his life he was going to challenge a prey with more than fangs and claws to fight back.

Chandler had never faced a prey with guns before.

The thought filled him with dread.

THIRTEEN

A score of conflicting thoughts raced through Chandler's mind as the horse gradually made its way down the devilishly tricky trail toward the sound of the river. The closer he got to the water, the louder it became and the harder it was for the hunter to hear his prey. Yet the infamous raiders had no fear and did not even attempt to subdue their voices.

Chandler leaned back against his saddle cantle and gazed at the dense terrain. It was impossible to see anything apart from the entangled green brush and tree trunks.

Before riding out of Rattlesnake, a handful of the survivors had talked to the young hunter. Chandler had learned how many raiders had attacked the remote settlement and had a vivid description of Corbin.

One of the old ladies in town had told him how

she had witnessed the indignity Molly had suffered at the hands of the rebel leader.

Chandler tapped his boots against the sides of his sure-footed stallion and tried to clear his thoughts for what he was quickly approaching.

Anger mixed with weariness made it impossible though.

All the hunter could see was the beautiful Molly being abused by someone who was meant to protect her. He gritted his teeth as the grey wove through the last of the brush at the foot of the rocks. He hauled rein and stopped his muscular mount.

Defying his own bulk, Chandler looped a leg over the neck of the grey and slid silently to the damp soil. The moist ground let him know that he was far closer to the river than he thought.

Chandler took hold of the reins and stroked the horse's nose as he tried to formulate a plan. Yet the hunter was not used to taking on eight heavily-armed men. The raiders had honed their notorious reputations over years and probably knew more ways to kill than he had even imagined possible.

He had always tried to dispatch his prey as quickly and painlessly as possible, but he knew that the wanted gang had no such compulsions.

By what he had observed back in Rattlesnake Valley, they enjoyed torturing their prey as much as they liked killing them.

Chandler began to lead his horse through the thick vegetation, wondering whether he really had a remote chance of bettering the men who had years of experience in slaying their enemies.

Death had never troubled the hunter. But now he knew it was only one mistake away.

In the wilderness death was the price all creatures paid when they made that mistake. As someone who was willing to place his life on the line every single day that he lived, Chandler realized that it could strike at any moment.

But facing eight men who relished killing in a way that was totally alien to him unnerved the big hunter. How could he fight such foes?

Then as he rounded a massive boulder and saw the river twenty feet away from where he stood, he remembered Molly. She was facing a fate that no female should ever face, he thought.

No matter how hard this was going to be, he had to do it to try and save her. After what Chandler had been told about Corbin's actions outside the school house, and the indignity he had inflicted upon Molly, the hunter knew he had no choice.

Even if he had never set eyes upon the handsome woman before, he would still have to intervene. That was simply the way he was made.

Men did not hurt womenfolk.

Men had to attempt to stop anyone who did. That

106

was the way he had been taught and he could do nothing to change that fact. Even mountain men had an unwritten code of honouring the fairer sex.

He stopped.

As he turned his head, Chandler heard the distinctive sound of noisy riders and their horses moving along the riverbank. Chandler screwed up his eyes and vainly attempted to see them, but the brush was too dense.

Then he looked at the muddy ground between the river and where he stood. Nine sets of hoof tracks marked the ground. Chandler bit his lip. He knew that they had passed here only a few moments earlier and were heading along the river's edge just as he had figured.

Chandler stroked his horse and forced the tall grey back behind a monstrous boulder. He would have to get ahead of them otherwise their mounts might catch his scent and alert the raiders, he thought. The breeze was blowing along the confines of the gorge.

Without a second's hesitation, Chandler hastily mounted and backed the horse into the soft undergrowth. He dragged his long leathers to his right and then tapped his boots.

The stallion began to move speedily through the tall undergrowth. Chandler turned the horse and rode up through the multitude of trees.

He hung over the cantering horse's neck as the grey gathered pace so that he was virtually invisible to any prying eyes that might catch a glimpse of him.

The sun was ebbing, and slowly but surely it was getting darker with every beat of his pounding heart. Unlike the merciless men he hunted, Chandler knew every part of the dense forest like the back of his hand. As he encouraged the grey forward, he had already worked out where he would have to travel to get ahead of them.

The black-tailed grey stallion moved like a phantom as it found the quietest route through the undergrowth. Chandler did not have any notion where exactly the infamous rebels were on their trek along the fast moving river.

But he knew exactly where he was headed. He had been there many times, but never to await such lethal prey. Chandler knew that there was a steep waterfall roughly two hundred yards away from where he had spotted their horses tracks.

The hunter considered the situation as the horse forged on through the rough terrain. Chandler knew that the waterfall would stop the rebels for the night. It was a dangerous place to try and negotiate even during the hours of daylight, let alone after sundown.

Strangers would never attempt to steer their horses down through the perilous array of jagged rocks to continue their journey until they could actually see hazards that had already claimed many lives. The drop was at least thirty feet and one false step could send even the most sure-footed falling to their deaths.

Massive boulders interspersed with splintered lumber would impale anything that fell upon them. The water surged over the rim of the falls and crashed over the slippery rocks before thundering down on to the white foaming rapids.

Chandler had avoided this part of the forest for years after making the mistake of underestimating how perilous it was to attempt the descent. It had taught him a painful lesson. Beneath his buckskins, his muscular body still bore the scars of that hard-learned lesson.

The hunter was well aware that the raiders were definitely headed for the open range. But even Corbin and his ruthless followers would be forced to halt for the night.

Chandler pulled back on his long leathers as he closed in on the waterfall. He stared through the moonlit mist and gazed down at the white rapids as water battled the mostly hidden rocks beneath the surface.

Chandler had only ever seen grizzly bears daring to enter the ice-cold river in search of fresh salmon leaping out of the frothy water and over the razor-sharp rocks. Only a bear could endure the freezing temperature of the water. Men who fell into the rapidly moving water did not survive for long unless they could scramble back out.

The grey stallion was now walking through the untamed undergrowth as Chandler closed in on the top of the falls. A massive tree defiantly rose out from between the boulders. Its sturdy branches loomed over the edge of the waterfall.

Chandler knew that normally this would be a perfect place to set traps but then realized that he would not be able to do so without endangering Molly. His mind raced as he tried to formulate another plan that might get the better of the rebels but not pose any threat to the beautiful school teacher.

No matter how hard he tried, Chandler just could not think of anything apart from a straight gunfight. The well-built hunter did not like the thought of taking on skilled killers for he knew that they were experts at what they did.

He was only a hunter.

Suddenly he heard them far below his high vantage point and held his stallion in check. He glanced over his shoulder in the direction that the sound had come from. Chandler listened harder.

His keen hearing could detect the small troop of riders approaching along the muddy riverbank.

Chandler bit his lip and looked around him as if desperately searching for inspiration. Soon he would have to decide on what he was going to do to save Molly without getting killed in the process.

Chandler urged the horse on.

FOURTEEN

There were few places as eerily quiet as the trail from Rattlesnake Valley to the vast open range. It wound its way from the remote settlement through the most hostile of forests to be found anywhere in the territory. Few men had ever ventured into the trees apart from the mountain men who had once thrived here. The range went on for as far as the eye could see, but it took determined riders to locate the massive expanse of land.

It was a total contrast to the tree-flanked town. It seemed that whereas the forested terrain was overflowing with every form of wildlife, the range seemed dead. Yet the range led to many far larger towns and that was the bait that drew so many men to attempt the crossing.

The rugged, almost flat, range was littered with

the sun-bleached bones of all those who had failed to get across its incredible width. Yet men still travelled this way.

Men who either had no fear of death or were simply a tad short on time to choose a far safer route. Corbin knew that the uncharted range was a dangerous option but, with enough water and supplies, he reasoned that they could cross in relative safety. For men who had left untold quantities of death and destruction behind them, Corbin knew that it was the only course they could take.

They had to head west.

They had no other options available to them but to continue westward. Their brutal tactics had branded their images into the minds of all those who had experienced the sickening acts they still employed.

There was no turning back for the eight Confederate rebels. Only death awaited them if they ever dared to retrace their tracks. The murderous savagery that had been encouraged during the war was now recognized for what it was. Sickening and grotesque butchery.

Their brutal actions had made it impossible for any of the rebels to retrace their trails and head back to where they had once lived. Now they had to keep going forward and that was what they reluctantly were forced to do.

Most of their war-time contemporaries had already fallen foul of the Grim Reaper and in the darkest regions of their demented minds the raiders knew that their own time was also running out.

Yet unlike decent folks, this only spurred the rebels on to inflict even more outrageous atrocities. None of them, not even Corbin himself, saw any reason to curb their scurrilous deeds.

In their sordid brains, if they were going to die, then so was every other man, woman or child they encountered. Morality no longer existed in them. They did not give a second thought to the things they did or what others thought.

That was why Molly was in so much danger. Colt Corbin and his henchmen were not only vicious killers, they were also unpredictable.

Chandler was fully aware of this.

The rebels had shunned the rule of law for so long they had grown to believe the rantings of their leader. It did not apply to them because, just like the country that had been victorious during the war, they did not recognize it.

What they wanted, they took. Whether it was the money inside a bank, fine horses to rustle or females to abuse or sell, they took it. Whatever they had once been, they were now little more than wild animals.

Corbin and his bunch had slaughtered their way from the battlefields of the south with no regard for those they encountered.

Yet animals never killed simply because they could.

Only men who lived lawless existences did that.

Chandler continued to ride on to where he knew the nine riders would be forced to stop for the night. The sky above the young hunter was changing colour with each beat of his heart.

As he glanced up through the entangled branches he noticed a glowing hue of crimson spread out across the heavens. It was a rare sight but one which men like Chandler recognized.

A wry smile crossed his young features as the grey stallion continued on toward the mighty tree that marked the highest point above the falls.

'Well look at that,' he whispered into the horse's ear. 'It looks like the gods are out to help us tonight, boy. We might just save Miss Molly after all.'

Like all men who risked their lives by hunting in the wilderness, Chandler was superstitious and believed in omens both good and bad.

As the grey reached the massive tree perched high above the waterfall, its master hauled rein and stopped it. A ghostly scarlet hue bathed the entire forest in its eerie cloak of blood-coloured moonlight.

A new confidence surged through his veins as the hunter studied the hostile terrain that surrounded him. Chandler quickly dismounted and rested his knuckles on his hips as his narrowed eyes stared at the almost red moon casting its strange light down across the forest.

It was a good omen.

It was a hunter's moon.

FIFTEEN

Massive boulders loomed in all directions like giant monsters surveying their prey. Defiant pines sprouted between the colossal rocks on the hillside and hung over the river beside the waterfall like ravenous vultures above the rocky trail that led to the eerie rim of the falls. But it was the increasing volume of sound that disturbed Colt Corbin as his mount made his way through the strange moonlight. The sound of thunderous water as it rushed over the falls and crashed into the unseen rocks far below was not only ear-splitting but also unnerving.

None of the riders had ever seen anything quite like it before as everything was bathed in the reddish hue. It was as though Satan himself had risen from the bowels of Hell and painted everything in blood.

'What in tarnation is going on here, Colt?' Trooper Bo piped up nervously as he clutched his

117

carbine across his grey tunic. 'Where are you taking us?'

'Trooper's right, Colt,' Fred Katt shouted above the sound of the waterfall. 'The sky ain't meant to turn red after sundown. It ain't never done so before. What's going on?'

Corbin did not answer the barrage of questions aimed in his direction. He had no answers. All he knew for sure was that he too had never seen a night sky with a scarlet moon before. His hooded eyes darted across the river, but the trees and undergrowth there were equally tainted.

'Why don't you tell them, Pa?' Molly taunted the wide shoulders of her father as she rode behind his long-legged mount. 'The great Colt Corbin knows everything. Tell them.'

Corbin turned on his saddle and glared through the strange light at her. He spat at the defiant female and then swung back and eyed the terrain ahead of them.

Molly lowered her head and smiled. She had read about the rare atmospheric oddity some called a blood moon while others referred to as a hunter's moon. It amused her to see the deadly eight rebels starting to become increasingly nervous by a simple trick of nature.

She had heard many of the stories concerning the forests that surrounded Rattlesnake. Some were utterly unbelievable, but others seemed to have just enough truth in them to raise doubts in even the most logical of minds. The riders who trailed her along the muddy riverbank were getting more and more anxious as the deafening noise of the waterfall grew louder.

The horsemen steered their mounts through the imposing landscape and continued to consume the whiskey they had stolen from the settlement earlier that morning. Hard liquor and frayed nerves were not a wise mixture.

The young school teacher had heard that the most frightening thing anyone can ever face is their own imagination. Molly knew that was where the true monsters dwelled and was determined to use it against them.

Colt Corbin glanced back at the terrified faces of his men and then at the smirk on his daughter's handsome features.

'What you grinning at, gal?' Corbin growled at his daughter.

'I'm just wondering why everything looks like its bleeding, Pa,' Molly lied. Her words had barely left her lips when she heard the men behind her start to get noisier.

'I know what your damn game is, Molly,' Corbin hissed as he pointed a finger at her accusingly. 'Don't think you can rattle their cages and get away with it.'

119

Molly fluttered her eyelashes. 'I don't know what you mean, Pa. I'm not doing anything.'

'You'll regret the day you were born when me and the boys are through with you.' Corbin turned back and stared into the mist that hung ahead of their horses. The strange sight made him forget his daughter as he stared at the swirling crimson mist. 'Look at that.'

Every eye stared at the constantly moving vapour as water crashed below the top of the falls and was then captured in the eerie crimson moonlight. None of the rebel outlaws had ever seen anything quite like it before. Their mutterings grew louder as they drew closer.

'What the hell is that, Colt?' Bodine bellowed.

'It's a curse,' Katt exclaimed. 'Where in tarnation have you brung us?'

Corbin glared at his daughter and then at his men.

'Quit your ranting,' he demanded. 'You're starting to sound like a bunch of old women.'

Molly dwelled upon her father's threats to her as sickening memories flooded back from the depths of her subconscious. She had remembered hardly any-thing until now. As the horses plodded through the mud, every outrage was suddenly recalled in vivid detail. Molly glanced at Corbin as the veil was lifted from her mind and she finally recalled the atrocities he had subjected her to. What her father had done to her when he had briefly returned when she had just turned sixteen was just the tip of the iceberg.

The smile faded from her handsome face.

A tear rolled down her cheek as she stared through the crimson moonlight at the monster who had defiled her at every opportunity.

Corbin looked at her and laughed.

'You've gone quiet, gal,' he taunted. 'About time.'

Molly wiped the tear away but did not respond.

SIXTEEN

Chandler had worked feverishly since his arrival at the massive tree that marked the very edge of the waterfall. He knew that he could not set traps as he would usually if he were after wild boar, bears or mountain lions. The possibility of hurting Molly made the idea of setting traps impossible. Yet there were more ways to catch large game than just hiding steel jaws around.

The hunter always carried three coiled ropes when he set out into the forest and knew exactly how to use them. For twenty minutes he had been carefully rigging the entire area with a series of looped nooses which he silently prayed would capture the deadliest of game.

Then he had removed his hunting rifles from his saddle and methodically placed them at strategic points in and around the boulders and trees.

Chandler knew that any of his rifles had the power to take down an eight-feet-tall grizzly and ought to be able to handle Corbin and his followers.

Each of the twin-barrelled rifles was loaded with buckshot and trained down at a single spot close to the river's edge. All he had to do was move stealthily through the forested undergrowth and squeeze their triggers.

He checked his Bowie knife and then made sure that his .45s were fully loaded and ready for action. As he led his grey stallion away from where he assumed the raiders would empty their venomous bullets, he heard the sound of the horsemen as they reached the very edge of the falls.

'They're here, boy,' he whispered into the ear of his mount as his hands secured his reins to a tree branch. He patted the horse on its neck and then turned back. 'I sure hope I get to meet you again when the gunsmoke has settled.'

His eyes narrowed.

Now it was time.

Time to take on the eight murderous creatures. Creatures that were far more dangerous than any of the wild animals he had ever hunted before in the vast forested hills. Time to face not only their wrath but also attempt to rescue Molly from a fate he could not even imagine.

The young hunter removed his heavy top coat and

hat and spread them over the saddle of his trusty mount. He flexed his massive frame in readiness for what he knew was about to happen. He rested his hands on his holstered gun grips.

Chandler took a deep breath and silently began to move through the dense brush. With each well-placed step the thunderous waterfall grew louder, but it was the unmistakable sound of the approaching horses that he was listening to.

He looked up through the entangled tree canopies at the large red moon that loomed over him and touched his brow in silent salute.

With his hands gripping his holstered six-shooters, Chandler continued on toward the noise of the horses. He moved quietly toward what he believed might be his death. And yet, unlike the depraved men he was about to face, the hunter had something they did not have.

Just like the mythical Sir Galahad from ancient tales, Chandler was pure of heart and driven by nothing more than the desire to rescue the beautiful Molly, even though he believed she did not even know of his existence.

SEVENTEEN

Corbin had now reclaimed that which he believed belonged to him and was considering which punishment would be the best to teach his wayward daughter a lesson that she would never forget. Molly had made the mistake of thinking that just because the secret service had given her a new identity and moved her to the remote settlement of Rattlesnake Valley, she had seen the last of her father and his scurrilous henchmen. Nothing could have been further from the truth.

Men like Corbin never relinquish what they believe to be their property. In his eyes, Molly belonged to him. Even though he had no paternal feelings for her, he knew from lurid experience that she might have other uses.

The mist over the rim of the falls was even thicker as Corbin led his followers to what appeared to be the end of the trail. He hauled rein and stared at the muddy ground and then noticed a small clearing to his right.

'We'll make camp here,' he announced before hoisting his leg over the cantle of his saddle and lowering his weary frame to the ground.

The expression on the faces of his men was almost exactly the same. They too studied the area and then glanced down at the powerful man who was leading his mount away from the river.

Katt dismounted quickly and tossed his empty whiskey bottle at the fast-flowing water.

'What the hell is going on?' Katt raged pointing at their surroundings. 'Where have you led us to, Colt? Look at this place, it ain't nothing but a dead end.'

'No it ain't,' Corbin disagreed.

Trooper Bo and a handful of the other men dismounted behind Katt and started to stare at Corbin with the same nervous look in their eyes.

'What you mean, it ain't?' Katt snarled as he closed the distance between them. 'You've led us up this damn river to a place there ain't no way out of.'

'There's a waterfall yonder, Colt,' Trooper gasped as he moved as close as he dared to the falls.

Corbin tied his long leathers to the branch of a tree and then sat down on a fallen tree trunk. The eerie light made Corbin's eyes seem almost demonic.

'I ain't deaf, I know there's a waterfall there,' he drawled before pulling out a cigar from his pocket and biting off its tip. 'So what?'

'So what? How are we meant to keep heading to the range?' Katt snarled pointing at the eerie mist. 'Our horses ain't got wings. We'd have to fly over them falls to keep heading west.'

Corbin scratched a match with his thumbnail and cupped the flame to his cigar. He slowly puffed and then flicked the match at the mud.

'We'll keep going after sunrise,' he said through a line of smoke. 'There ain't no point carrying on unless you can see where you're stepping.'

'But the trail ends right here,' Bodine argued. 'There ain't no more trail, Colt.'

'There's always a trail, Jango,' Corbin snapped.

Suddenly Molly spoke.

'I hate to agree with my father, but there usually is a trail if you look hard enough to find it,' she said from her high-shouldered horse. 'We can't see it now but once the sun rises I'll bet we'll find it.'

The eight men swung on their heels and faced the straight-talking female. She sat astride the tall horse staring down at them with the same defiant look her father always favoured.

Corbin inhaled smoke and raised an eyebrow. 'Molly seems to have more guts than the rest of you put together. She knows I'm right.'

Katt rested his hands on his holstered weaponry and glared at the man they had regarded as their leader since the end of the war.

'What if we're being trailed, Colt?' he asked. 'We're trapped here if a posse comes after us. This is a dead end and I don't cotton to being trapped in a dead end.'

Corbin rose back to his full height and gripped the cigar between his teeth. He strode toward his men and they parted as he knew they would.

'There's no way that anyone could follow us from that stinking little town, boys,' he stated. 'You killed all the horseflesh there. Even the most determined of critters couldn't trail us without a horse.'

The raiders looked at one another sheepishly and considered the words Corbin had just spoken. They knew he was right, but that did not help them feel any less vulnerable.

'I guess he's right,' Trooper Bo shrugged. 'There weren't a horse left living when we rode out of that town. Nobody could trail us from there.'

Bodine rubbed his unshaven face. 'I guess so.'

Corbin was not as confident as he sounded, but knew that when his dwindling troop were liquored up, it was best to stand firm. He filled his lungs with more smoke and then cast his eyes up at Molly.

'What we need is grub, boys,' Corbin said loudly as he eyed his daughter thoughtfully. 'You're gonna cook for us, girl?'

Molly slowly nodded.

EIGHTEEN

For his size, Chandler was incredibly agile. In his profession it paid to be flexible if you wanted to get the better of the various wild animals in the forest. Using his powerful upper strength, his muscular arms pulled him up the trunk of the enormous tree perched on the very edge of the waterfall. The reddish moonlight mixed the night time shadows and cast the entire area in an unholy hue. The sturdy branches, which seemed to defy gravity, were suspended over the deadly watery abyss.

With one of his saddle ropes coiled over his shoulder, Chandler continued to climb up the damp tree trunk until his boots found one of the branches. He stopped and moved out along the nine inch wide branch using further offshoots of the tree to maintain his balance. The rich summer foliage gave the hunter good cover as he tentatively made his way through the rising spray to where he had a clear view of the notorious Corbin raiders.

Six feet away from the safety of the tree trunk, his keen eyes spotted them in the clearing below him. They were at least thirty feet away from where he stood upon the branch.

Chandler held on to an overhead branch as he peered through the small gap in the thick leaves. He could not hear a single word the outlaws were saying due to the constant thundering of the water as it crashed down into the rapids far below him.

His eyes narrowed and tightened as they searched the figures below him for Molly. Then one of the men struck a match and put its flame to a pile of kindling. Within seconds the dry kindling erupted into a fire. The other outlaws placed logs and branches on the flames until they had a good campfire going.

As the flickering light of its flames danced around the clearing, Chandler saw her. The tiny female looked utterly different to the school teacher he had secretly admired since she had arrived in the remote Rattlesnake.

Molly Drew, as Chandler knew her, looked like someone who already knew her ultimate fate and had resigned herself to it. The hunter clenched the fist of his free hand as he watched her move like a phantom around the blazing campfire.

'Don't you fret none, Miss Molly,' Chandler muttered under his breath. 'I'll do my best to save you from them godless critters. I promise you.'

Even though he knew full well that she could not hear anything he was saying, the hunter felt better for making his solemn vow to the defenceless female. He slipped his arm from the saddle rope and began to uncoil its length. With every movement of his heavy body on the slippery branch, the rope grew longer.

Chandler had the makings of a plan burning like a branding iron inside his head, but was fully aware that if any of the infamous bunch spotted him now, it would be all over. It was said that any one of the raiders could shoot the eye out of an eagle, and Chandler had no intension of testing the theory.

He carefully lowered himself down until his legs straddled the wide branch he had been standing upon. As he sat on the branch his hands worked feverishly and threaded the rope through its lasso loop.

Chandler tightened the loop and held on to the slack.

The rope was over forty feet in length. He pulled the leaves away from beside him and stared down at the clearing intently again. He licked his dry lips and then swallowed hard.

He wondered if the rope was long enough.

He also wondered if the branch was strong enough to take his weight. Seeing Molly had spurred the usually easygoing hunter into doing something which he never did.

Chandler was about to take risks that could cost him his life if something went wrong. Common sense screamed for him to wait until the outlaws bedded down for the night, but he knew that would be too late.

Far too late.

As Molly prepared a meal by the blazing fire, Chandler could see the expression on the faces that surrounded her. He had seen that look before on the faces of lustful men who were liquored up and eyeing a bar room girl back at Rattlesnake.

Every one of Corbin's raiders had that exact same look on their faces as they watched Molly rustling up their supper. Chandler glanced at the older man that he presumed was Corbin himself.

Even Corbin had the same sickening look on his rugged face as he watched his daughter. The young hunter rubbed the knuckle of his thumb across his gritted teeth as his mind raced.

Like sand cascading downward in an hourglass, time was running out fast. The determined young hunter realized that Molly's fate lay in his hands. No matter what, he had to risk everything to get her away from the rebels before they ravaged her like the rabid wolves they reminded him of.

Seeing her face again bathed in the light of the hunter's moon had fuelled his resolve. Chandler knew that he would have to act quickly if he were to prevent the outlaws from having the defenceless Molly for dessert.

She was like a lamb surrounded by drooling cougars. The young hunter knew that if he did not act soon, Molly did not have a chance.

Chandler had rigged the entire area with his hunting rifles and expertly looped ropes. All it would take to start the chain reaction of his carefully calculated fireworks was courage and big heap of luck. He had prepared a lot of traps around the clearing before the nine riders had arrived. Traps that he had set to work in a precise sequence. There was little room for error and Chandler knew it.

The last thing he wanted was for Molly to get caught in the middle of the mayhem he was about to unleash. Chandler realized that if Molly were to panic when the trouble started, she could get wounded or even killed.

Neither option appealed to the hunter.

Chandler balanced on the branch and continued to watch the dark-haired Molly from his precarious vantage point as she continued to prepare her captors' meal.

The last grain of sand had drained from the hourglass. Chandler knew that there was no more time. He had to summon all of his courage and dive into the abyss and pray that everything went as he had planned.

Chandler wrapped the tail end of the rope around his arms and checked that the rest of the coil was unheeded. His powerful hands tugged at the knot that he had secured to the branch as his eyes stared down into the darkness below his feet.

He could not see where the fast-moving river water was hitting the jagged rocks but he could hear it. The chilling noise of thousands of gallons of water sounded like the roars of some gigantic beast.

Terror surged through his large frame, yet it was not for his own safety; it was for the handsome female in the clearing beside the campfire. Chandler knew that he was her only hope and that weighed heavily on his massive shoulders.

He filled his lungs with the icy air and carefully took another step along the sturdy branch. The bark was damp under his boot leather. Damp and slippery. He steadied himself and gripped the rope as firmly as he could.

Before he lost his balance completely, Chandler rocked back and forth as if summoning every last ounce of his immense strength.

Then like a fearless mountain lion he blindly threw himself out into the crimson vapour. The spray burned at his eyes as he swung through the air.

All Chandler could do now was pray that the hunter's moon would bless him as he swung helplessly on the rope as it hastily uncoiled.

NINETEEN

Chandler clung to the damp cutting rope and fear-lessly swung out over the cascading falls, through the crimson vapour until the rope tightened. Then the hunter felt his body being catapulted back through the moonlit spray toward the branches of the huge tree and its foliage. Chandler raised his boots as he hurtled through the icy air above the perilous drop.

The thunderous sound of the constant falling water masked any noise that the hunter's actions might have made. The momentum was far faster than the young hunter had imagined, yet there was nothing Chandler could do except hold on for dear life.

The first that any of Corbin's raiders knew of the intrepid Chandler's unexpected appearance was when he came hurtling through the lower branches of the massive tree and swung above the boulders at the very edge of the clearing.

Chandler held on to the rope with one hand as the rope once again tightened. He pulled one of his six-shooters from its holster and then dropped behind several boulders close to the river's edge.

In a matter of seconds, Chandler had emerged from out of the satanic mist and fallen like a stone on to the damp ground. Yet the drop had not gone exactly to plan, and Chandler had hit the rocks hard. The jagged edge of one of the standing stones had caught one of his boots and torn through his buckskin pants. The young hunter knew that he was bleeding badly as he tumbled into the gaps behind the large rocks.

He dragged his boot free of his grazed foot and pulled his bandanna from his neck. He mopped up the blood and then tied the neck scarf tightly around his calf.

His sudden arrival had not been noticed by all of the men seated around the campfire. Only three of the startled onlookers had seen Chandler's daring feat.

They stared in disbelief at where he had suddenly appeared and then vanished from view. One of the witnesses was the rebel leader himself.

Totally astonished, Corbin had spat his cigar from his mouth and then risen to his feet. He dragged one of his trusty repeaters from its holster as his men also scrambled to their feet. Only the few men who had been facing the waterfall had any notion what had alerted Corbin.

'Did you see that?' the gruesome rebel leader shouted at his men. 'Did any of you see that?'

Every single one of the raiders raced to the side of their shaken leader and stared toward the rim of the falls. Some had not seen anything, but still clutched their six-guns as Katt moved ahead of the bunch and glared into the eerie scarlet mist.

'I seen him, Colt,' he drawled in nervous tone.

'You seen who, Fred?' one of the rebels piped up.

Katt pointed his drawn Colt at the rocks beneath the tree and poked the air with its barrel. 'I seen a real big fella come flying from out of the mist and dropping down behind them rocks yonder.'

'Sounds like you got a gut full of bad whiskey, Fred,' Joe Snape chuckled. 'It ain't possible for a man to come flying through the air.'

'I ain't drunk, Joe,' Katt insisted. 'I seen what I seen.'

The outlaws who had not witnessed the incredible feat frowned at the snarling Katt. It seemed totally unbelievable, even to those who had spotted Chandler's impressive arrival.

Katt's words only confirmed what Corbin knew to be true. He moved through his men angrily. His eyes darted at each and every one of their faces and silently dared them to disagree. His look alone muted their voices as he stared hard at the boulders.

'Look yonder at them falling leaves, boys,' he snapped, before swinging around on his heels to look at them again. His eyes were like the strange moonlight. They seemed almost red as he contained the fire that burned in his innards. 'They're falling coz a mighty big fella in buckskin just came crashing through them. If any of you knuckle-brains want to argue about that, just tell me.'

Jango Bodine pushed his way between his cohorts toward Corbin and nodded at the irate rebel leader.

'I seen the varmint, Colt,' he confirmed as he too glared at the edge of the waterfall and the huge rocks which littered the ground beyond the clearing. 'He dropped just behind them boulders.'

Trooper Bo nodded in agreement and then sniffed the air as he caught the aroma of burning. He glanced over his shoulder at the campfire.

'Where in tarnation has that gal gone?' he blurted out as flames consumed the contents of the skillet.

Corbin angrily pushed Trooper aside and looked toward the fire. The witless rebel was correct. Molly was nowhere to be seen. The feisty female had taken advantage of her captor's confusion and fled into the forest.

Furiously Corbin spat and shook his head.

'Damn it all, that little vixen has high-tailed it,' he

growled angrily and kicked at the muddy ground beneath their boots. 'She also burned the vittles.'

'We'd best go looking for her, Colt,' Bodine said. 'She's way too valuable to let run off.'

Corbin turned and moved back to the shoulder of Katt.

'We got more important things to fret about,' he drawled before returning his glare to the rocks as the light of the campfire licked their smooth surfaces. 'I'm wondering who that hombre is out there and what his intensions are.'

'But what about Molly?' Bodine interrupted.

'She won't get far,' Corbin said. 'Not in this forest at night. When we catch her again I'll let you all teach her a lesson. One she won't ever forget.'

Katt nodded. 'Now that sounds mighty good.'

Corbin pushed his way through his men and glared at the rocks as he pondered the identity of the man he had witnessed doing the seemingly impossible.

'Molly can't hurt us none, boys,' he said dryly. 'I ain't so sure about that bastard though. I'm wondering who that *hombre* over yonder is.'

'Are you sure it was a white man?' Snape sneered. 'It could have bin an Injun.'

The other three raiders started to chuckle.

'A flying Injun?' one of them blurted.

'There ain't no Injuns around here anymore,' Katt argued.

Corbin snorted as he cocked the hammer of his gun and pointed it back at the boulders. 'Whatever that varmint is, he's over there waiting to pick us off one by one.'

'But what about your daughter, Colt?' Trooper Bo wondered aloud as he scratched his head.

Corbin's eyes darted at the rebel. 'I already told you. She can't get far, Trooper. We'll round up Molly after we teach that buckskin that it don't pay to come uninvited to our camp.'

Katt looked at Corbin. 'How come that critter ain't started shooting at us, Colt? I don't get it.'

'Maybe the bastard broke his neck when he landed behind them rocks, Fred,' Bodine smirked. 'I sure hope he did. There's nothing I hate more than a lucky galoot. Swinging through them trees and not breaking you're neck is just plumb annoying.'

Corbin gestured at the disbelieving rebels standing behind Trooper Bo. He waved his gun at them and then pointed at the rocks.

'You boys can go rustle the critter up,' he ordered.

Joe Snape tilted his head at Corbin.

'Why us?' he asked. 'Why d'you want us to go looking for that varmint, Colt?'

Faster than spit, Corbin raised his cocked six-shooter and pressed its barrel into the temple of the rebel. A cruel grin etched Corbin's face. His icy stare drilled into the heartless soul of the terrified outlaw.

'According to you, there ain't nothing to be feared of, Joe,' Corbin snarled angrily. 'You boys reckon that I'm seeing things that ain't even there. Prove me wrong.'

'But there might be some galoot hiding over yonder,' the rebel raider gulped. 'We could be wrong.'

Corbin continued to glare into the eyes of the man.

'You four boys are going over yonder to kill that buckskin coz none of you believe he exists,' he hissed like a sidewinder ready to strike. 'Any objections and I'll shoot you for disobeying orders, Joe.'

Joe Snape gulped. He knew that Corbin never bluffed. He had seen the rebel execute several of their number over the years for disobedience. He nodded.

'OK, Colt,' Snape stammered and signalled to the three outlaws behind him. 'We'll go kill that varmint for you just like you told us.'

'Good idea,' Corbin said dryly as the four men readied their handguns and began moving toward the boulders. 'Saves me killing you.'

TWENTY

The hunter lay winded beside the boulder where he had landed a few minutes earlier and rubbed his ankle frantically. The tightly knotted bandanna had stemmed the flow of blood but it still trickled between his fingers. He stared through the reddish gloom at the skin he had torn as his massive bulk had collided with the rocks on his way to the ground.

Pulling his boot back over his grazed foot, Chandler silently cursed before hearing something out in the clearing that flushed all thoughts of his injury away. The sound of a snapping branch had alerted his hunter's senses that someone was walking from the campfire to where he was secreted.

Chandler bit his lower lip and crawled along the gap between the boulders until he was able to get a glimpse at the approaching four men.

'Hell,' he cursed. 'They must have spotted me.'

143

His heart started to pound inside his chest. He scratched at the soft ground and found what he was searching for. It was the end of one of his ropes that he had carefully placed there earlier. He brushed the soil and leaves aside and lifted it.

'This had sure better work,' Chandler whispered as he watched Joe Snape leading the three other wanted men toward the rocks. 'If it don't, I'm in deep trouble.'

Saying a silent prayer, Chandler summoned all his strength and tugged the rope as hard as he could. Suddenly all hell broke loose in the clearing beside the fast flowing river.

Massive flames erupted from the undergrowth as buckshot came blasting from the barrels of his hidden hunting rifles and cut through the moonlight to either side of the four outlaws.

All four of the advancing rebels spun on their heels as deadly buckshot carved into them. Droplets of blood splattered into the moonlight like precious rubies. They floated in the air for what seemed an eternity before showering over the stricken outlaws.

The stench of gunsmoke filled the air as two of the rebels fell lifelessly into the mud. Their wounded cohorts staggered for a few moments and started shooting wildly as death slowly encroached on their stricken souls. Their bullets ricocheted off the boulders as they succumbed to the buckshot and dropped on to their knees.

Faster than he had ever moved before, Chandler swung around the side of the smooth boulder and fired his six-shooter at both men.

Tapering flames of lethal lead cut through the moonlight and hit Snape and his fellow raider in their chests. Both men crumpled into the ground. Gore spread out from the four carcasses beneath the mysterious hunter's moon.

Chandler's hunting skills had not let him down. Yet he felt no sense of satisfaction as he reloaded his smoking six-gun. For the first time in his life, he had turned his weaponry on his fellow man.

It did not sit well with the young hunter, yet he knew that Molly's life was at risk and he had no alternative but continue his quest to rescue her from the hands of Corbin and his merciless followers. Chandler returned the chamber back into the body of the gun and rubbed his sweat-soaked face.

Chandler rolled over and scrambled back to his feet. He rested his back against the towering boulder and then threw his body over a massive tree root. The hunter had barely landed when he heard the ear-splitting sound of gunfire across the clearing.

The four remaining rebels had opened up with their arsenal of handguns and furiously started to fire at the fleeting glimpse of Chandler.

Bullets tore through the air as Corbin and his

three men fanned their gun hammers. Chandler lay on his back as the hot lead passed just inches above him.

He felt the heat of the bullets as they narrowly missed his large bulk. Chunks of bark were torn from the tree root sending clouds of sawdust up into the strange scarlet hue.

Somehow Chandler had managed to avoid the bullets that came at him like a swarm of frantic hornets at incredible speed. He ducked and dived like a prize-fighter and then cleared another of the trees exposed roots as even more wood was blasted from the tree limb.

Chandler desperately tried to catch his breath.

His mind raced in search of his next move. He cocked the hammer of his .45 and returned fire. For every bullet he fired it seemed that four came in reply.

Lumps of bark and debris were carved from the tree above him. As he fired the last of his bullets, Chandler swiftly shook the casings from his gun and pushed fresh ammunition into the smoking chambers.

'This is getting damn dangerous,' he told himself as he fumbled with his six-shooter. 'A man could get hurt doing this for a living.'

His large hand brushed the smouldering sawdust off his buckskin jacket as another volley of bullets embedded into the tree trunk just above his head.

Chandler tried to think as more bullets hit the tree.

Their shots were getting closer, he thought. Too damn close for comfort. He turned over on to his belly and crawled around the tree trunk. With the huge width of the tree between the hunter and his enemies' bullets, Chandler started to get back to his feet. Suddenly his left boot slipped on the soft muddy soil.

For a moment, Chandler felt himself falling.

His razor-sharp reactions burst into action, and he holstered his gun and grabbed at a dangling vine beside him. Then his feet slipped off the muddy surface and he found himself suspended in mid-air.

The hunter hung for a moment and then looked down at the watery grave he knew awaited one more mistake. Using every scrap of his upper strength, Chandler pulled his heavy body upward until his boots managed to find a foothold.

Chandler clambered up on to solid ground and crawled away from the edge of the waterfall. He rested on his knees for a few moments before he heard the gunmen shouting to one another from the clearing.

With his nose pressed into the ground, the hunter knew that even though they were still firing their six-shooters in his direction, they could no longer see him. But the depraved Corbin was still trying to out-flank the unknown hombre who had somehow managed to reduce his already dwindling band by half.

Chandler steadied himself behind the massive trunk of the tree and tried to think. He had not imag-ined that he would get this far or last this long against such a formidable bunch. He had one trap left, but doubted that his luck would hold out long enough for him to spring it.

He had to try though.

Molly deserved that, he told himself.

Sweat trailed down his face as Chandler continued his seemingly impossible quest. He launched his large frame six feet to his left and clambered through the mud and rocks away from the massive tree. The entangled undergrowth might have slowed the average person, but not Chandler.

His determination carried him on regardless.

Unseen by the rebel guns, Chandler crawled on his hands and knees through the bushes to where the last of his traps had been set.

Never before had Colt Corbin lost so many of his followers in one swift stroke. He could not under-stand who the solitary man was or why he was risking his neck and taking on his infamous troop of rebels.

The grim-faced Corbin and his last three Confederate rebels moved cautiously toward the dominant tree and large boulders. Smoke trailed from their gun barrels as they closed in on the bodies of their dead comrades.

Corbin dropped on to one knee beside the corpse of Snape and turned it over. The light of the hunter's moon made the body look even more hideous. His eyes then darted around the area in search of the attackers. Katt held his six-shooter at hip height as he stood above the brooding Corbin.

'I reckon there must be at least three of them, Colt,' he suggested as he too looked nervously around the clearing. 'I saw scattergun fire come from both sides. Whoever these varmints are, they seem to be working together.'

Corbin straightened up.

'I reckon you're right, Fred,' he seethed furiously. 'I got me a feeling that we're up against a mighty strange bunch and no mistake.'

Trooper Bo and Bodine searched the dense undergrowth for whoever had fired the fatal shots as Corbin stared at the unearthly mist that moved like the ghosts of their fallen cohorts.

The rebel leader holstered his six-gun and then dragged his sabre from its scabbard. Moonlight danced along its honed edge as Corbin went to step over Snape's body.

'Come on, Fred,' he snarled. 'Let's kill the varmints.'

Suddenly Trooper called out from the under-growth. As Bodine raced to the side of Trooper, both Corbin and Katt turned and started to head across the mud toward the excited rebel.

'I done found me a shotgun, Colt,' Trooper Bo said as he pulled the large weapon from the under-growth. 'This gun has bin rigged to fire without anyone being within spitting distance. There's a rope tied to its triggers. One tug and this baby fired both barrels.'

Corbin and the others stared at the shotgun and then around the surrounding area.

'What's the betting that there's another scattergun rigged exactly like this'un over yonder?' Katt suggested confidently. 'I reckon that buckskin-clad hombre is all on his lonesome. He set a trap for us before we even got here.'

Corbin rested the blade of his sabre on his shoulder.

'That ain't possible,' he said. 'We killed all the horses in Rattlesnake before we left. Who could have gotten here before we did? This don't add up.'

'Who in tarnation are we dealing with here, Colt?' Trooper asked nervously as he looked around the area, which was still bathed in the haunting colour of gore. 'And what would he want with killing us?'

Corbin stepped away from the others.

'A bounty hunter after our reward money,' he surmised confidently. 'We're worth a lot of money, boys. Somehow a bounty hunter got on our trail and laid these traps to kill us after we left that stinking town.'

Bodine shrugged. 'It still don't add up, Colt. But I can't think of nothing better than it being a bounty hunter.'

'It has to be a bounty hunter after the reward on our heads,' Katt nodded. 'There just ain't no other answer.'

Trooper pointed at the stout tree.

'That's the last place we seen him, boys,' he drawled as he reloaded his six-shooters. 'I'll bet he's still there. All we gotta do is go and kill the critter.'

Corbin grinned and ran his thumb along the gleaming edge of his sabre blade. 'You boys can shoot him and I'll chop his damn head off his shoulders.'

His three companions nodded in agreement.

'You gonna gut him, Colt?' Trooper grinned eagerly. 'You gonna gut him like a fish?'

'Damn right, Trooper,' Corbin snarled. 'Damn right.'

FINALE

Chandler was crouched in amid the dense thicket of trees and undergrowth with his hand gripping the end of his last rope as his narrowed eyes watched the four men standing less than thirty feet away. Sweat still continued to defy the falling temperature and traced a route down his youthful features.

Without taking his attention from the four deadly rebels, Chandler searched his thoughts. Unlike the men that he was observing, he did not like the taste of killing men. Yet no matter how hard he tried, he could not find another way of stopping them.

The raiders would kill or be killed.

Chandler knew that he would have to do the same.

He rose back to his full height and squinted through the bushes at them as they moved back toward the rocks where he had landed less than five minutes earlier.

Neither Corbin nor the last of his men knew it, but they were doing exactly as Chandler had anticipated. They were walking into the last of his traps.

Chandler could not believe his luck.

Nothing ever went this well, he thought. Something was about to go wrong and he knew it. He gritted his teeth as his sweating palms toyed with the end of the rope. Chandler kept watching the men move across the clearing toward the rocks, waiting to spring his final surprise.

The thought of what might happen should he mistime this last surprise filled him with dread. He knew that they would turn their guns on him given half a chance to do so.

The hunter moved forward and peered through the bushes that had hidden him from their keen eyes since he had reached the thicket.

As Corbin and his three fellow gunmen stepped over the blood-soaked bodies of their comrades, Chandler hauled back on the rope.

Suddenly the soil around the advancing rebels erupted into a blinding haze of flying dirt. The rope which Chandler had laid a few inches under the surface of the clearing rose swiftly like a spring.

A series of large loops coiled around Bodine and Trooper Bo and lifted them off the ground. Both men were propelled upward and then came crashing down into the ground heavily.

The sound of their breaking bones was even louder than the crashing waterfall. Corbin and Katt swung on their boots and stared to where the rope led into the undergrowth.

They aimed their guns straight at him.

Just in time the hunter dived to his left as Fred Katt fanned his gun hammer. The blinding flashes of the .45 spewing out its avenging venom lit up the clearing.

Branches were torn from the bushes above Chandler's prostrate body as he feverishly crawled for cover. The hunter reached some saplings and drew one of his Colts.

'I knew that wouldn't work,' Chandler muttered as he rose back to his full height and rested his back against the thin straight tree trunks.

Then Katt got lucky as he peppered the undergrowth with bullets.

One of his stray shots hit the hunter in his back. Chandler arched in agony as he felt the bullet enter his shoulder blade and burst out of his chest. The gun fell from Chandler's hand as pain rippled down his arm.

Then he heard Katt racing toward him.

He stooped and was just about to pluck the gun off the ground with his left hand when Katt came crashing through the bushes behind him. Before Chandler could react, he felt the impact and went

154

flying into the ground. Katt grabbed hold of Chandler's bloody shirt and turned him over. Then he sent a powerful punch into the younger man's jaw. Half dazed, Chandler raised his good arm and grabbed the rebel's face. The two men wrestled but with only one good arm the hunter was no match for Katt.

Another crushing blow smashed into the hunter's face as the infamous raider clambered on to Chandler's chest. Punch after punch flew between the two brawling men.

Then Katt grabbed Chandler's throat and started to squeeze with all his might. The hunter grabbed the rebel's wrist and forced it away from him. He kept twisting Katt's wrist until the rebel released his grip.

Then Katt pushed the still smoking barrel of his gun into the face of the man beneath him. The barrel was red hot and burned Chandler's flesh.

'Say your prayers, buckskin,' Katt snarled and pressed the barrel of his .45 against the side of the hunter's temple. The dazed eyes of Chandler looked up at the grinning man atop him.

Katt squeezed the trigger.

A click filled both men's ears as the hammer fell on a spent bullet casing. Chandler grabbed the surprised Katt by the throat and threw him with all his force at the blood-stained saplings. As the wounded hunter got back to his feet, he saw the outlaw's face glare at him as Katt began to reload the gun.

Chandler got to his knees and then drew one of his own guns just as Katt cocked his weapon's hammer. Both men raised their guns at precisely the same moment. A blinding flash erupted from Chandler's gun. The bullet hit Katt dead centre.

The outlaw fell on to his face. Startled, the hunter stared down at the body at his feet.

'Hell, that was close,' Chandler mumbled before he staggered to the bushes and looked into the clearing at the brooding Corbin.

The rebel leader was standing with his sabre in his hand as though readying himself for an impending duel. The moonlight flashed along the blade as the snarling Confederate squared up to where he had last seen his underling disappear.

'Come on out here, buckskin,' he raged. 'Or are you afraid to face a man with a sabre?'

With his gun gripped firmly in his hand, the severely wounded Chandler defied his own giddiness and walked from the bushes into the moonlit clearing. Blood flowed from the hole in his chest, but that did not stop the hunter.

He closed the distance on himself and the infamous rebel.

'How come your guns are holstered?' he slurred as he tried to keep his six-shooter aimed at Corbin. The trouble was the .45 grew heavier with every drop of his blood.

Corbin did not reply.

'Who the hell are you, buckskin?' Corbin questioned the young hunter.

'My name's Chandler,' the hunter replied as he kept advancing on the infamous Corbin.

'Are you a bounty hunter?'

'Nope,' Chandler stopped and took a deep breath. 'I'm just a hunter. An ordinary hunter.'

Colt Corbin's expression altered as he tried to fathom out why a hunter would take on his notorious band of raiders. He gripped the large sabre in his hand and studied his adversary with a look of disbelief carved into his scarred features.

'If you're just a hunter,' he growled, 'Then how come you risked your damn neck taking me and my men on? Answer me that.'

Chandler swayed as his mind filled with a sickening fog unlike anything he had ever experienced before. He was becoming weaker fast. He staggered and tried to focus on Corbin. It was impossible. His eyes no longer were able to see clearly as his brutal wound started to take its toll.

'I came to rescue Miss Molly, Corbin,' he managed to say before his legs buckled and he fell to his knees. 'I seen what you and your rebels did to the folks back in town. I came to save her from suffering the same fate.'

'You sure spilled a lot of blood trying,' Corbin laughed loudly as he saw the six-gun fall from Chandler's hand. He began to walk toward the helpless young hunter with his sabre clutched in both hands. Chandler could do nothing except watch his advance.

'I reckon I failed her,' the hunter sighed heavily as he felt his strength evaporating with every breath. 'I should have stuck to hunting critters that don't shoot back.'

Corbin glared hatefully at the helpless hunter knelt before him. 'You've killed my troopers, boy. I'm going to have to punish you for that.'

Chandler raised his head and looked at Corbin.

'How'd you figure on doing that?' he asked.

'Simple,' Corbin grinned. 'I'm gonna separate you from your head. That'll learn you.'

Chandler resigned himself to the inevitable.

Then as Corbin raised the large sword above his head and prepared to bring it crashing down on the hunter's neck, a shot rang out and echoed around the clearing.

The sabre fell from his hands as Corbin rocked on his heels and staggered backwards toward the river. Somehow Corbin managed to stop and dragged both his guns from his holsters. As his thumbs dragged their hammers back, another shot rang out.

This time the bullet was lethally accurate.

Corbin was lifted off his feet and fell into the fast-moving river. Within seconds, the limp body was washed unceremoniously over the edge of the water-fall.

Chandler stared through blurred eyes at the unmistakable figure of Molly as she walked from beside the campfire with a smoking Winchester in her hands. She tossed the rifle aside and then dropped on to her knees beside the wounded hunter.

She pulled a canteen off her shoulder and unscrewed its stopper. As Chandler accepted the ice cold drink of water, he felt her comforting arm around his shoulder.

'You'll be OK now, Lane,' her voice soothed him. 'I'll fix your wounds up.'

It was as though he were staring at a dream. He smiled at her handsome face and then realized that she had called him by name.

'You know my name?' he weakly asked.

Molly pulled his head into her shoulder. 'Sure I know your name, Lane. I've been waiting for you to speak to me ever since I arrived in Rattlesnake Valley.'

'I didn't think you'd want someone like me talking to you, Miss Molly.' He blushed coyly.

'You were wrong.' She stroked his jaw. 'Very wrong.'

Chandler took her hand. 'You shot your father for me.'

She shrugged. 'I had to. Otherwise he'd have decapitated you, Lane.'

'I've an inkling that he'd have chopped my head off as well, Miss Molly,' Chandler sighed.

She smiled and touched his cheek. 'When you've rested I'll take you over to the campfire and tend to your wounds, Lane.'

Chandler patted her hand gently. 'I'm obliged.'

Molly placed her lips gently on his temple and kissed him.

'You're welcome.'